ADVENTURES ARE EVERYWHERE

Short Stories for the Explorer at Heart

Elizabeth Horst

To Titus and Gabriel

May you never hesitate to follow the adventures that have been living within your hearts since the very beginning.

Table of Contents

A Note from the Author

Who can resist a good adventure? As a child, I recall living in a constant daydream filled with ordinary people like you and me who passed the time exploring how to perform heroic feats worthy of great honor. My free time was either spent wandering through the outdoors in search of the curiosities of nature or curled up inside with a good book where I could disappear for hours. That pattern continued well into my adolescent years and has even stayed with me today, although my journeys and daydreams look quite different now.

To be an explorer of any sort necessitates a type of willingness to go beyond the realm of what others expect you to do and set yourself up for attention, both supportive and critical. Some adventures take us to astonishing places, while other journeys merely challenge our way of viewing the world and suggest a new way for us to face it.

Whatever your lot in life, I hope you take the time and space to explore. Start with yourself, discover your true passions in life, and then move on out from there to consider the world around you. How can you make the world a better place because you are in it?

At the end of the day, we can all be heroes on a grand adventure, though each one of us is unique and our own journey will look different from anyone else's. After all, most real heroes aren't found wearing capes, flying through the air, or standing in the limelight to enjoy well-earned praise. Real heroes are found in the background, facing the challenges and cleaning up the messes that no one else wants to deal with.

So, I ask you, what kind of explorer are you? Let the adventures begin!

Elizabeth Horst

May 2024

1
Robbery at Doonesville

It was a dry and windy Sunday morning in the southern part of Doonesville. The whole town's population of forty-two people had turned out early, and forty-one of those souls were now sitting in the meetinghouse at the center of town, listening to the circuit rider Father Brown preach mightily in the pulpit. An occasional "Amen" came from the graybeards in the far right corner, but for the most part, the congregants were silent and still in their pews.

The only soul not in attendance for Sunday's meeting was an old reprobate sitting on the stoop in front of the general store. He shifted a bit in his baggy brown trousers and leaned his matted gray head against the porch railing as a dust cloud began to gather at the head of Main Street. Sighing with the wind, he tilted his grizzled chin back and began to let out the quavering beginnings of an old sailor's tune.

"Fifteen men on the dead man's—"

His voice trailed off as the cause of the dust cloud became apparent. Two riders were steadily making their way down the street past his stoop, headed directly toward the meetinghouse. Sitting up straight, the reprobate followed the strange men with his eyes, noting their old clothes, their ratty hats, and their tired horses. He craned his neck all the way around to watch them until they disappeared around the corner of the large white building.

"Trouble," muttered the old man, leaning back again and shaking his head. "No good." Sighing again, he folded his arms across his chest to ward off the brisk wind that swept along the road in front of him.

"Must be the whiskey." Eying the empty bottle that sat on the steps beside him, he shook his head again and resumed his toneless warbling, completely dismissing the sight of the two riders from his memory.

Around the corner of the meetinghouse, the two newcomers dismounted from their steeds and tied the reins to the hitching rail alongside several other horses and a couple of carriages. After a brief consultation, they nodded in agreement, removed their dusty hats, and began to rustle in their saddlebags for holier garb.

"Do you s'pose the old reverend is done yappin' by now?" Frederick asked, looking down his crooked nose at his companion before disappearing as he pulled a black robe over his head.

"'Spect so," Oscar replied. "Filcher tole me he'd be done promptly at 9:45, and here it's 'most 10."

The latter speaker pulled a beat-up timepiece from his front pocket and eyed it a moment before holding it up to his ear. Hearing nothing, he shook it a bit, took another listen, and then replaced it in his shirt with a careless shrug. Glancing up at the sun and then down at his shadow, Oscar nodded to Frederick with confidence.

"Then let's go," Fred growled, straightening the ratty cloak around his shoulders and turning to see his friend doing likewise with his own robe.

The two travelers met Deacon Strong in the alcove, finding him neatly replacing a stick with a rabbit's foot in its special ledge by the bell pull trapdoor.

"Ahhh," the deacon breathed a wispy greeting, clasping his hands in front of him and bowing slightly. Whether he was nervous, uneasy, or simply startled, the men did not know, but they imitated his peculiar behavior by also clasping their hands in front of their own robes and bowing back.

In actuality, Deacon Strong was giddy with delight. It was collection day at the parish and the poor box was simply brimming over with generous gifts. His busy mind had been occupied all sermon with purchases for the needy and improvements to the building. Now, unclasping his hands, he motioned the men to follow him as he opened the sanctuary doors before them.

As the three crossed the threshold, the parish man swiftly surveyed the congregation, wondering how to seat the two men in such a way that it would add to the harmony of the church and not cause the least bit of division. At the same time, Deacon Strong noticed that Father Brown was just returning the cup to its place on the communion table and dearly hoped that the newcomers would not disrupt the meditative mood of the service.

Before the deacon had a chance for his worry to set in, Father Brown turned to face the congregation, lifting his hands to pray a simple two-line blessing.

"Amen," all the people responded, and Frederick and Oscar eagerly echoed the word, causing Deacon Strong's heart to swell with happiness that the travelers were doing their part to fit in with the assembly. Clasping his hands together once more, he bowed his head in solemn and reverent prayer.

As if on cue, the old pump organ began to wheeze out an eerie tune and all the people stood in unison to sing. Presently, the instrument came to life with a rush and hastened to catch up with the voices, the blended sounds creating a glorious symphony that reached into the rafters before filling the entire building.

Slowly, the voices began to fade one by one as astonished eyes met the sight of a black-robed figure solemnly parading up the aisle toward Father Brown. By the time a second figure appeared in a dingy blue robe, all the congregants were simply standing there with their mouths agape. The only remaining sounds came from the pump organ and Father Brown, who shared a holy "Amen" before also coming to a rest.

Father Brown raised his bespectacled face from the Psalm book and lowered his conducting arm to find himself flanked by two strange men. He blinked in surprise as the taller man in the black robe stepped forward to shake his hand vigorously. Then the stranger turned toward the pulpit, lifted down the poor box, tucked it under his arm, and spun about on his heel to march down the aisle.

Before anyone could raise a note of protest, the shorter man in the blue robe also stepped forward and took Father Brown's hand in both of his in an apparent move of joy and thanksgiving. Turning toward the congregation and lifting Father Brown's arm in a movement of celebration and praise, he began the following prayer:

"We praise Thee, O Lor' our Father, for Thy generosity an' goodness that these gifts shalt verily bless Thy poor people of Shaftesbury who suffereth from a ragin' fire."

A great gasp was heard through the room at this juncture and many a compassionate head was shaken in pity as the speaker continued unabated.

"An' we thank Thee, O God our Lor', for these good folks who giveth abundantly at all times. So let all people that on earth do dwell sing praise to Thee, a hundred times o'er."

With a hearty "Amen and amen," the organist and Father Brown immediately took the cue and began to lead the singing of the Old Hundredth.

The building shook with fervor as the blue-robed man walked back down the aisle in a great meditative state to meet his companion who was busily bowing to and wringing the hand of Deacon Strong. By the time the song ended, the men were on their way. The wind blew the door shut, leaving the deacon all alone in the alcove to adjust the tuft of hair on his head.

Father Brown set down his Psalm book and lifted his hands to pray over the people one last time before delivering the benediction. All heads dutifully bowed in response, except for one that belonged to a certain man by the name of Albert Jenkins.

This fellow carefully scanned the small crowd suspiciously until the last "Amen" was pronounced. Then he skirted the little groups of congregants as they busily gathered around the Father. He plucked the sleeve of another young man who stood near a group seeking to console Deacon Strong in his grief over the plight of Shaftesbury. The furrow in Albert's brow smoothed when he saw the thoughtful look on the face of his friend.

"You thinkin' what I be thinkin'?" Albert wondered as the two of them escaped the hot confines of the meetinghouse and headed for their horses. Dusting off his hat, he set it firmly upon his head and looked at his friend for a reply.

"Ain't been no fire in Shaftesbury of late," Elias Swift said, his normally jovial expression now sobered. "Else, I would have heard of it."

"True word!" Albert said angrily. "And holy day or not, I mean to get to the bottom!"

Elias tightened the saddle on his horse and patted her neck gently before swinging himself up with an easy movement. "Meet you by Duncan's Corner in half an hour!" he said cheerfully. "I'm off to equip my little peashooter!"

"Half an hour?" Albert said in surprise, knowing he was at least a 15-minute ride from his home. "But what about food and water and—" He stopped with a cough as the dust set a-swirling from the hooves of Swift's horse caught him full in the face. Sneezing and snorting violently until he sounded more equine than human, Albert finally escaped from the cloud of dust. He found a woman holding a small child in front of him—both of them staring agape in wonder.

Recovering himself fully, he inclined his head politely and touched his hat's brim. "Ma'am. Baby," he acknowledged one after the other. Turning toward his own animal, he leaped into the saddle and quickly set off for his homestead without delay.

At high noon, when most townsfolk enjoy a quiet midday meal and consider how to best celebrate their peaceful afternoon, Albert and Elias were in hot pursuit of the strangers across the open plain.

They rode a good mile toward the plot known as Tommy's Field, but greedy Thomas Thatcher had died long ago, and his poorly built shack crumbled just last winter. Now, a pile of rough boards and rotting slats served as the last landmark and memory of that skinflint of a man.

The two mounted horses thundered by, leaving a dust trail behind them. A line of trees ahead marked a change in terrain from the rolling fields and dusty flats of Doonesville to the rocky, pine-covered barrens of Steuben. Beyond that lay the windy slopes of Shaftesbury, serving as the outermost region of Hog's Head County, which was curiously shaped like a pig's face with snout, ears, and all.

The two men slowed their animals to an easy trot by the grove of hardwoods that led to the Stony Brook in order to examine the area for clues about the direction that Frederick and Oscar had taken.

"Curious thing," Albert murmured, pointing to the bank of the creek. "Hoof print," he explained as his friend turned in the saddle to look.

"Gettin' a drink, no doubt!" Elias said cheerfully, urging his horse forward to take a quick mouthful of the bubbling water. Looking ahead, he motioned toward higher ground. "They went on that-a-way, for certain."

"Let's go," Albert said impatiently, nudging his own horse back into a quick walk. They rode one after the other along the bank until the brook turned sharply to the left and they both saw signs that led up into the rocky slopes.

"They're takin' the overpass!" Elias said in excitement. "If we take the shortcut, we're sure to find them in Dooley's Dustbowl!"

"But they've got a whole hour on us," Albert protested. "We'll never catch up that way."

"My good Nellie can do it," Elias countered. "How's your ratty nag?"

"Ratty nag!" Albert shouted in disbelief and then offered a challenge. "Lead on, you rascal! Hob Nob Bill and I will teach you and your filly a fine lesson!"

They started off again at a steady pace over rocks, around trees, under vines, kicking up more dust the whole while. They made good time, too, though it was not quite clear at any point who was leading the way or winning the challenge. Before long, the two young men spotted two large rocks ahead, knowing that their shortcut would soon end at the lookout to the famous dustbowl.

"There!" Albert suddenly shouted, catching sight of two additional riders, nearly startling his gelding and sending the two animals off again on a wild pursuit down the rough trail leading into Dooley's Dustbowl.

Elias also was excited and took out his revolver with a great grin, waiting until they were closer to the strangers before firing a warning shot into the air.

Oscar and Frederick and both of their horses were so overtaken by fright that all four of them went flying in different directions, or nearly so, but the men recovered themselves quickly so they were not unseated from their horses. Their tired nags, however, could not withstand another hard run and stopped altogether after seeing the pursuing riders, giving Elias an easy advantage to cut in front of Oscar and seize his horse's reigns.

Frederick, still holding the poor box under his long black robe, was desperate to escape and tried to whip his horse into a trot. But just when the old nag began to move forward and the thief thought he would have a fair chance, there was Albert with his own revolver neatly pointed at Fred's nearest eyeball.

"Mind your manners, before I lose mine," Albert said with an angry stare, forcing Frederick to reluctantly pull his tired horse to a halt.

Attempting to appear noble, Frederick sat straight in the saddle and looked at both men one after another. Finally, he demanded in a solemn tone, "Why dost thou stop two goodly priests on their way to deliver the poor folk of Shaftesbury from the woes of their tempestuous calamities?"

When Elias and Albert recovered themselves from laughing, they noticed at once that Oscar's face was turning as colorful as that of a fine red beet, and then they turned back to face Frederick.

"Friend," Elias said in a jovial tone, "two problems with your high and mighty sermon."

"One," said Albert, "Shaftesbury is to the west, and we're headed north."

"Two," continued Elias, "no pile of money ain't gonna help people who have nothing to buy with it."

Seeing the error of his logic, Frederick's face also became tinged with red and he was silent after that. After another moment, seeing how expectantly Elias and Albert watched him, he reluctantly began to hand over the poor box, but not without a bit of a pout and a sniffle of defeat.

Triumphantly, Albert and Elias dismounted and then forced their prisoners to clamber from their own horses, though still at gunpoint. They searched the men and their horses, but besides a couple of handguns that only had two bullets apiece, Oscar's battered pocket watch, the two ratty cloaks that served as bedrolls, and some moldy breadcrumbs, they came out empty.

In a last-ditch effort, Frederick attempted to jump into the saddle of his captor's horse, but Albert still had a grip on the reins and Elias's last name of Swift was a sure reminder of how well he could withdraw his little peashooter.

Presently, the small party set back off for Doonesville—Elias back on Nellie and Albert upon Hob Nob Bill with the poor box safely stowed away in his saddlebag with the two sorry thieves trussed up atop their own tired horses.

It took some time to return to town and the clock tower pointed well beyond four o'clock when the riders finally walked up Main Street, past the general store, and toward the little telegraph office, which was where the jail cells were located. Doonesville, after all, was not large enough to have its own sheriff's department and so the telegraph office served as the most convenient location to house prisoners until the proper authorities could come by to take care of such criminals.

As the procession passed the general store, a number of eyes followed with amazement. The old reprobate was long gone by this time, having returned to his stables to uncover a secret stash of whiskey, but a couple of boys were sitting on the stoop and gazed after the men and horses with curiosity and delight.

One lad, whose father ran the telegraph office and kept the key to the jail cells, immediately leaped up and ran home to tell his parents about the news. The other boys also rose, but to follow the dust trail all the way down to Mr. Simon's office, watching as Elias and Albert helped the prisoners down and began to consult each other about the next doings.

"Here, Johnny!" Elias suddenly called out to the eldest of the three watching boys. Elias was only a few years older than the particular lad in question and knew him well, grinning as Johnny walked up with great eagerness.

"You take these sorry nags to the stables and give them a good rub-down for the night!"

Johnny and his friends all came forward at that point, only too glad to help, considering themselves an incremental part of the heroic acts of the day. For weeks after, they bragged about that day to their other friends, claiming to have found curiosities of all sorts on the horses and their saddles—innocuous claims to be certain, but silly and false all the same.

The tired beasts having been led away for a restful evening, Davis Simon the Third came puffing up with his two sons in tow—the younger returning after delivering the message and the older having come along with his father from the house.

Miles, the elder, stood with Elias and listened to the whole tale as his father and Albert locked the thieves away and provided them with several rough comforts to make their stay easier.

"We'll have Father Brown speak with you after night service," Davis told the two as he locked the bars and the office door behind him. Pocketing the keys, he shook his head and followed Albert back to the horses.

"I'll never know," he admitted, "what causes men to act like beastly thievers."

"Desperation!" Elias offered.

"Perhaps," Albert said, remembering the moldy bread, lack of bullets, and ratty cloaks. "But sure ain't no excuse."

"By no means," Davis agreed.

Elias and Albert took up their horses' reins and made as if to mount so that they could return to their respective homesteads.

"Well, see you at night meeting," Albert called over his shoulder, thinking that he had but one hour to return home, get his chores in, have something to eat, and then return.

"No, but stay!" Davis said quickly before they could mount. "We were sharing a mouthful before night service. After the good work you both have done, you've earned your share of the pickings, and then some."

"Thanks," Albert said, greatly relieved. He looked at Elias who was also tired and hungry, and grinned at the invitation.

"I'll just slip the poor box to Deacon Strong first," Albert added, lifting off the heavy saddlebag from his horse. "It will give him somethin' special to praise the Lord about."

"Good word!" Elias replied.

So, they all set off to the meetinghouse and then to Simon's, feeling tired but happy as they looked forward to a great evening of rejoicing for the entire community.

As for Oscar and Frederick, they sat in jail all that night, and the next, and for quite some time to come until the matter could be discussed among the town and county authorities. They were none too happy to have their freedom so restricted, but they never had to worry about eating moldy bread on the trail or wearing out their bedrolls.

Their only trouble at present was the old reprobate, who haunted them at all hours of day and night to gloat over their imprisonment. Apparently, that old man was less relieved by the fact that the Lord's money was back where it belonged, and more giddy than he had ever been in his life because two people in the town appeared to be more wicked than he!

2
The Gold Maps of Adamsville

Tales from Buck's County, Part I

Adapted from an original screenplay called "The Gold Maps" by Green Tree Films, owned and operated by MD Horst.

The year was 1859 and it was a beautiful spring morning in Coatestown, Buck's County. On a hill that lay above the Running River, a rough manmade structure stood in the middle of a small clearing. The birds were singing and the squirrels were hurrying around in search of their morning breakfast. Two men lay on the floor of the shack, fast asleep, with their belongings sprawled all around them.

The first man, a fellow named Peter Ramsey of about twenty-two years of age, stirred slightly and then realized that it was morning. Sitting up, he rubbed his face vigorously and then looked over at his companion, a younger man who wore a patch over one eye from an accident when he was but a teen.

"Robert, get up," Pete said groggily, reaching for his hat. When he did not get an immediate response, Pete prodded his partner again. "Come on, Robert! You're too lazy. The sun's already halfway up." Correcting himself, he added, "Well, it's a quarter up."

Struggling to his feet, Pete headed to the opening of the hut and peered up at the sky. "Get to the fire."

"All right," Robert Bentley finally responded in a sleepy voice. "Just a few minutes." He was also a young fellow in his early twenties and felt that he was entitled to more sleep, but the day would not wait.

"Come on!" Pete said in irritation, bothered by the fact that he always had to nag and prod the younger man. Approaching the fire pit, he looked down at it and scowled. "Robert! You let the stupid fire out again!"

Robert was finally awake. "Well," he said in his lazy drawl, "you know how people forget."

"No, I don't know how you forget!" Pete said angrily. Walking down into the fire pit, he kicked the charred logs and then pulled his hat down on top of his head. Seeing his companion stumble out of the hut, he changed the topic.

"Well, anyway, I'm robbing Mr. Brown's today."

Robert scrunched up his face, his one good eye blinking in the bright sunlight. "Who's that and why you gonna rob him?" he demanded. "He doesn't have anything special!"

Pete shrugged violently as if he could not be bothered by trivialities, but then he explained patiently, "He lives over on Johnstown Street in Adamsville, and haven't you heard? He has a watch that's made of pure gold."

"Oh, yeah," Robert said in sudden excitement, "that person all the town talks about!"

"Yeah," Pete said, beginning to feel quite pleased, "and he has a ring that's made of the finest silver."

"Well," Robert said in a whiney tone, "why can't I go with you?"

Pete faced his younger companion directly and replied firmly, "You gotta make a nice breakfast after letting the fire go out!" Seeing the defeat in Robert's attitude, Pete grinned and readied himself for the task that lay ahead.

"I'll see you later," he said, striding off through the woods.

"All right," the younger man said in a grumpy tone underneath his black hat and eye patch. "I'll have a delicious breakfast ready." He muttered to himself for a bit and decided that if Pete got to have fun, then he deserved to have more sleep. Rising, he stumbled back into the hut and lay down on his grubby blanket for a nice nap.

Robert's snooze turned out to be a half-hour long, and he suddenly awoke with the dreadful realization that Pete would be expecting a delicious meal as promised. Rushing about in desperation for a few minutes, he sank down beside the fire pit, grumbling noisily to himself about why he had agreed to the difficult task.

But then Robert was struck with a wonderful idea! Jumping up, he started running through the woods with his giddy thoughts swirling about like last fall's leftover leaves blowing around his boots, all until he tripped over a log and rolled halfway down the hill, landing near a rock by a barbed-wire fence.

"Here it is!" he said, looking around and gasping for breath. "Mr. Jackson's!"

Getting up slowly, he added with a bit of a scoff, "It's smaller than I expected." Robert passed a cow that stood near the fence, who looked at the trespasser mildly, and then headed down into the little farm toward a chicken coop that stood next to a spacious garden.

Robert's merry thoughts were brought to a quick halt and his feet skidded to a short stop as he spotted a black dog lying down on the lawn not too far away.

"Oh no," he said to himself, always in the habit of talking aloud, "it's Jackson's guard dog!" Crouching down behind a tree, he muttered, "They say that dog is vicious!"

Cautiously, the thief snuck over toward the chicken coop, but just as he was about to slip around the corner of the pen, he tripped on the hitch that was used to move the coop and promptly fell into the mud.

The chickens immediately squawked, alerting the dog!

Terrified, Robert sprang for the coop door, flipped up the latch, and leaped inside, desperately hoping that the dog would not spot him. The chickens continued to squawk noisily as the canine trotted over and sniffed all around, even peeking into the crack in the door. Not seeing or smelling anything unusual, the dog soon trotted away, with some apparent disappointment.

Robert waited just a moment and then slipped out of the coop with obvious relief, going around to the back of the pen to open up the egg door. He thought about what a close call he had faced as he nabbed a couple of eggs from the nest and then made sure to close the door before making fast tracks across the lawn back to the woods. In no time at all, the thief was hurrying back up the hill and returning to his shabby hut.

Approaching the fire pit with great satisfaction, Robert let out a sigh of relief, thinking of Pete and how pleased he would be. He said aloud, "Fresh eggs!" and laid them down on the ground gently. Straightening up, Robert went inside the hut to get his frying pan and tinder to restart the fire and cook up a delicious breakfast.

In the meantime, Pete spent quite some time trekking all through the woods on the opposite side of their hill as he headed toward the Town of Adamsville to find the residence of one Mr. Edgar P. Brown. It was a good three-mile hike and he felt hungry, tired, and worried about the weather. Glancing up at the clouds that suddenly shadowed the morning sun, Pete accidentally ran into a log and tripped over it, rolling down a small knoll that led to a stream bed, one of the many overflows that came out of the hilly Lone Pine District.

Hastily crossing the stream bed and getting his boots wet, Pete complained aloud, "Where's this confounded house?!" Climbing up the knoll on the other side of the stream, he peered off into the distance, one way and then the other, each in turn. Then he noticed a finger of smoke from a house toward the north and immediately headed in that direction.

After a bit further, Pete finally came to a great sprawling house surrounded by grassy lawns. Hiding behind a big bush, he stared around in all directions and then rushed across the first lawn to take refuge behind several other trees.

Gazing all around at the rich man's property, he eyed the house again and grinned. "A beauty it is indeed!" he told himself with comfort in his tone. "Mr. Brown should be at work! No complications!"

With that, Pete quickly ran across the lawn, though he glanced back and forth in all directions to make sure that no one was in sight to spot him. As usual, his attempts to run and look at the same time resulted in him nearly falling into a small ditch, but he quickly recovered himself with the help of a young maple, the last tree between him and the mansion.

Pete felt impatient as he rushed across the last stretch of lawn up to one of the windows and began to examine the frame for an easy way to lift the outer screen. His brief attempts were fruitless and he stopped in frustration, slapping his palm to his sweaty forehead in desperation. The jolt to his brain, however, brought an idea to him.

A grin spreading across his face, Pete remembered aloud, "My father always said, 'A fork's better than a screwdriver!'—sometimes." Pulling out a fork that he kept in his pocket, he used the tines to raise the outer window. Satisfied with his work, Pete proudly tossed the fork over his shoulder and then pushed up the inside window by the heavy panes. Boosting himself up on the frame a bit awkwardly, he struggled to get inside and then wondered about whether he should be continuing to act in such a way at his age.

Now in the house, however, Pete quickly put the trials of the window behind him and began to look around the room. He had entered what appeared to be a small but roughly furnished parlor with three doorways. He crept across the dark carpet up to each door in turn, peeking into the adjoining rooms carefully, but then decided to take the middle door, for it led up a mysterious narrow stairway to the second floor of the house.

Pete's boots made the stairs creak something terrible, but he slowly persevered to the top and found another small room with even more closed doors! He was used to making such decisions by now, and so he followed his hunch about the very furthest doorway, approaching it and slowly turning the handle.

Opening the door, Pete found a large and cozy bedroom with multiple beds and a wooden desk and chair against one wall. Quite satisfied with his discovery, Pete looked about the bedroom.

"This place is definitely nice," he told himself, and then noted the desk again with a growing sense of delight. "There's something nice in there," he predicted, the visions of a gold watch and a silver ring beginning to dance inside his greedy mind.

Going up to a little kerosene lantern and matches that sat on the desk, Pete lit a match and then adjusted the wick carefully before lighting it, but he still managed to burn his fingers in the process. Blowing on his fingertips, he dismissed them from his mind and opened the top of the desk, beginning to look through all the little drawers and doors in search of treasure. He pulled on the little knob of a tiny little door in the middle of the desk and a delighted expression shone across his face as the brilliant magnificent of a gold watch glittered right in front of his eyes! Taking off his hat with respect, Pete gently lifted the watch out of the desk and examined it in great admiration.

"Such a beauty!" he exclaimed aloud in awe. "Pure gold! Just wait until Robert sees this—his eyes will probably get as big as apples! Just look at this beauteous gold!"

Suddenly, out of the corner of his eye, Pete spotted another item in the desk and nearly dropped the watch in his amazement. Reaching back into the desk through the little doorway, he lifted out a fine ring between thumb and fingertip. The golden ring glowed in the lantern light and Pete's blue eyes shone like stars.

"I thought this was going to be made out of silver," he exclaimed, mesmerized by the ring. "But even better—pure gold! Made of the finest!"

Pete's astonishment and awe had not quite reached their peak. Again, he spotted another item, but this time it was a piece of paper folded up in one of the slots next to the little door. Carefully putting down the ring beside the watch, he reached out with trembling fingers, wondering if it was truly what he imagined it could be. Delicately taking out a piece of paper and unfolding it, Pete gazed down and read it aloud.

"The Gold Maps of Adamsville!"

With awe and delight on his features, Pete quickly lifted the gold watch and looked at its face. Satisfied that he had ample time to study the map, he pulled up a nearby chair and sat down to examine the markings in detail. Immediately, and to his delight, he recognized the very first landmark—Rocky Mountain Road—and so passed a good amount of time reading and re-reading that precious map in an attempt to figure it out.

That very same afternoon, at 1:45 PM, Mr. Brown was taking a pleasant stroll along his road back to his house. He was a very particular and punctual fellow, and every work day from 9:00 AM to 2:00 PM, he could be found in the Town of Adamsville, managing his assets and employees over a leisurely luncheon. Ordinarily, he was a generous man with those who also shared his values for hard work and pleasant conversation, but he tired quickly of people who tried to befriend him for his money, and he hated those who tried to openly rob him of his hard-earned goods.

Thinking about all of this as he looked forward to a good afternoon of work from his home office, Mr. Brown cast a look across his property and smiled. But then he spotted a shiny object in the grass on his front lawn and stopped in amazement. Walking up to the very spot, Mr. Brown bent down and picked up a solitary fork!

"What on earth?" he said aloud, looking at it closely. Glancing about here and there for another clue, Mr. Brown's perplexity began to shift into definite suspicion. He was certainly not the type of man to be chucking forks around on his front lawn! Then, catching sight of the open window before him, he hurled the fork back upon its place on the lawn and charged toward the window. He was most definitely not the type of man to leave his windows open, either, and a great feeling of panic seized him as he thought about the repercussions of a common thief creeping through his window into his house and stealing his golden watch!

Climbing through the window and finding the door to the stairway open, Mr. Brown's suspicions were immediately confirmed. Charging up the stairway, he caught himself and became crafty. Going quickly but quietly to his office door, he listened at the keyhole closely. Inside, he heard the curious sound of a strange man muttering to himself.

"I'm not going to show Robert this," came the voice. "It is my secret! I'll keep the gold myself." Then there was an evil chuckle and the sound of rustling paper. But then there was a wistful sigh and the man said in admiration, "Ha, such a beauty!"

At that, Mr. Brown had heard enough. Slowly opening up the door, he saw a strange man with a tan hat staring at him in horror.

Pure rage coursed through his blood and Mr. Brown hurled himself down the stairs into the office, screaming, "Don't you touch my gold, you little rat!"

The startled thief did not know how to react, giving Mr. Brown a clean advantage to attack him head-on. But poor Mr. Brown was not used to fighting and the impact caused him to fall down as well.

Seeing that, the thief laughed in an evil voice. "You wanna fight?" he demanded, putting up his fists, feeling that he had a sudden advantage.

But as small as Mr. Brown might be in comparison to the surly thief, his energy and courage had no bounds. Gathering up all his strength, he shoved the thief into a corner of the room and began to punish him.

"This is for touching my ring," he declared, giving the fellow a solid punch, "this is for touching my watch," and another punch followed, "and this is for touching me!"

But at the last punch, the thief recovered his senses and began to fight back. The men scuffled about for a bit, but then the thief decided to beat it. Hurrying for the stairs, the thief was well on his way out of the room when Mr. Brown tackled him, but only managed to take hold of the stranger's leg as the slippery fellow was desperate to get away.

The thief squirmed and kicked, and though he lost his boot in the process, he escaped from Mr. Brown's grasp! He hurried down the stairs with the homeowner in hot pursuit. Then the thief sprang out the window and all Mr. Brown could do was to reach out and grab at him desperately.

Again, missing his mark, Mr. Brown only managed to seize the fleeing man's tan hat instead of his shirt collar, his arm, or anything else that was more securely attached to his person.

The thief whirled around at that and seized the hat back with a bold and impudent laugh. "That's mine, thank you!" he shouted, and then rushed off across the lawn into the nearby woods.

Mr. Brown was exhausted, but furious. "The sheriff will hear of this!" he screamed after the thief from the open window. Too tired to follow, he closed each window securely and then went back upstairs to put his watch and ring into his safe.

The thief, who we know as Pete, ran and ran until he could run no more and then landed in the mud in exhaustion. He rested there for a bit, catching his breath, and pondered over the morning.

"Every time I've robbed before, I've brought something back," he thought to himself in great disappointment. "But not this time."

Then Pete remembered the map. "I have something better than I've ever brought before!" he thought in excitement, reaching for his back pocket and drawing out the Gold Maps. "I'll keep this to myself," he decided, tucking it back into his grubby belt and getting to his feet. He stumbled about in awkwardness, not having two boots to protect both of his feet and had no other choice but to limp the long hike back to his shack.

Some time later, Pete arrived at the hut to find Robert fast asleep by the fire pit with his hat tipped over his head. Angrily, he kicked at his partner.

"Sleeping again?" he shouted. "You let the fire go out!"

Robert sat up and squinted up at him, replying in a surly tone, "It's a well-earned nap after risking my neck to get you breakfast!"

"Breakfast," Pete scoffed, knowing that the time for breakfast had long passed. He was more in the mood for a fine dinner, but Robert was pointing to the frying pan that had long turned cold.

"Look! A breakfast fit for a king!"

Pete sat down on a nearby rock and picked up the frying pan. "Risking your neck indeed!" he said, studying the fried eggs and bread. "You probably stole it, and it was easy pickings!" He lifted one of the eggs and sniffed it gingerly.

"Me, on the other hand," he went on, seeing that Robert was looking at him curiously, "I was so close to being caught that he even took my boot!" He lifted his leg slightly to reveal a grungy sock for inspection and glared at Robert.

Deciding at last to get a word in, Robert said in a cautious tone, remembering his close call at the farm that morning, "Have you ever seen Mr. Jackson's dog?"

Ignoring that question, Pete stared at the bread and then hurled it at Robert in irritation. "Moldy bread!" Turning back to the frying pan, he looked at the eggs with sudden relish. This was food, even if it was poor pickings, and he was ravenous.

"Come on, eat it, eat it," Robert coaxed him on, having heard enough of his partner's complaining.

Agreeably, Pete took a big bite of the egg but found it so detestable to his palate that he immediately spat it out, wishing there was a way to scrape the taste off of his tongue.

"You must be the worst cook on this side of the Mississippi!" he said angrily, hacking and coughing.

Shrugging a bit, Robert replied, "There's a drop over there to wash it down."

"Thank God!" Pete proclaimed, though he had little faith to show, and immediately reached for the bottle, chugging down a couple of mouthfuls.

"So," Robert said slowly, wishing to get on to the more important things of life, "how'd the thieving go?"

"The thieving?" Pete said in surprise, putting down the bottle. "Well, I didn't get a thing!"

"Oh, is that so?" Robert cast a look over Pete carefully and then said in a crafty tone, "Well, that's funny. You always get something."

"Yeah, not this time," Pete said, his voice surly, though he was inclined to laugh because of his easy deception. Brushing off his palms, he set the bottle aside and rose. "Well, I'm going to get a well-earned nap just like you did."

"It's not well-earned if you didn't get anything," Robert objected.

"Ha!" Pete scoffed, knowing that both of them were plenty inconsistent and illogical in turn.

Tired of hanging around and doing nothing except drinking and sleeping, Robert slowly stood to his feet. "I'm going to go to town to get some food that's worth eating."

"Where are you going?" Pete demanded.

"Shabby's Hardware," Robert replied in a suddenly glum voice. "I hate that place, but it's the closest one around. That's what happens when you live in the middle of the rotten woods."

"Get some blankets and buy another boot for me!" Pete demanded from inside the hut.

Gearing up for the trip to town, Robert nearly tripped on the frying pan. Kicking it away viciously, he announced, "I'm off!" and then turned to run down the hill and across the field toward the little hardware store in Wolf Den.

From inside the shack, Pete chuckled to himself as he thought of his successful deception. Muttering to himself, he said in a greedy tone, "He thought I didn't get anything, but he's wrong! Gold Maps," he laughed in a contented voice. "And while he's in town, he's going to get me blankets for the journey! A boot to keep my foot dry! And some food that isn't made from that wretched cook!"

Casting a look outside the shack, he caught the sight of a striped kitten chowing down on the hateful fried eggs and said in disgust, "No one likes his cooking, except for that confounded stray cat!"

With that, Pete lay down with an evil chuckle and instantly went to sleep.

It was a late afternoon at Shabby's Hardware Store. Jeff Shabby was busily mopping up his desk with a rag and then tossed it away with some annoyance. It had been another slow day and he was bored. He studied an axe buried in a nearby log and then climbed up on his clean counter to examine the tools he had hanging up there.

Hearing the outside door creak, Shabby turned around to find a young man walking in.

"Great Jumping Jehoshaphat!" Shabby exclaimed with delight. "A customer!" Feeling instantly awkward, he jumped down from the counter and sat down on the opposite side on a rugged stool, attempting to compose himself. He peered at the man through his glasses from underneath his heavy eyebrows, recognizing him, but not remembering his name.

The fellow with the black hat and eye patch came up to the counter and said in a familiar tone, "Hello, Shabby,"

"Hey boy, how's it going?" Shabby replied, suddenly affable.

"Good." The fellow cast a critical eye around the store.

"What can I do for you?" Shabby pressed, rubbing his hands together in glee.

"I want two blankets and a boot," the fellow said in a straightforward tone.

At that, Shabby felt flustered again. "Two blankets—boots— well, all right—well, no—" Ceasing his stammering for a moment, he jumped over the counter to stand beside the young man. "So, blankets, and boots." Bending down to look underneath the counter, he picked up a pair. "Here your two boots are."

"I only want one boot," said the fellow in a patient tone.

Shabby started but then stuck a fingertip in his good ear to clear it out and then he swallowed and said slowly, "Did you say, 'One boot'?"

"Yes, sirree Bob," replied the fellow with a bit of a grin on his face.

At that, Shabby smacked himself in the face. "Extraordinary! A person who has one boot! That's crazy!" Then he asked, cautiously, "Um, left or right foot?"

At that, the fellow appeared a bit puzzled, but then he shrugged. "I don't care."

"You don't—extraordinary fellow!" Shabby exclaimed. He handed him one of the boots and set down the other on the floor. "There your boot is," he said in a satisfied tone.

"Thank you," the young fellow said politely. "And my blankets?"

"Um—oh! Right there!" Shabby picked up a rough-looking blanket from a nearby pile of farm equipment and smelled it quickly. It was not too badly off, but a freshening up and washing would do wonders. "Here, this would be 10 cents," he said, pointing to the boot, "and that would be 5 cents."

"Eh, two blankets, actually," said the fellow, appearing bored by this time.

"Ah, well," Shabby began to say, wanting to gingerly explain how an Indian chief had recently come in and bought out his supply, but then he caught sight of a blanket over the counter that he had neatly tacked up to hide the boxes underneath. Struck with a brilliant idea, he leaned down, ripped the blanket from the counter swiftly, and wrapped it up for the young fellow.

"Not a problem!" he said in excitement. "Another 10 cents."

At that, the young fellow searched his pocket and handed Shabby a coin. Then he picked up the blankets and the boot as the proprietor turned to put the money in the register.

Shabby felt happy. "So—" he began, turning around to strike up a conversation. To his surprise, the young fellow was gone! "Wait a second," he shouted, seizing a nearby axe. "You forgot to look at my axe! It's handmade, and the sled—there might be a late snowstorm!"

Seeing that all his shouting would not bring the fellow back to his store, Shabby sat down in a huff upon the counter. "No one ever buys anything cool here," he thought with great remorse and then pronounced aloud, "A shame!" Taking off his hat, he smoothed back his hair and his scruffy eyebrows. Glancing at his watch, he decided to close up for the day and go home for supper.

Mr. Edgar P. Brown was back in town that afternoon, but he was none too happy. Instead of a leisurely day at his home office, he had taken a wild ride down to Smithy and back and was very tired and sore from the unsuccessful journey. He thought about going home to his wife but was reluctant to go when he had no good news to give her. The more he considered the day, the more frustrated he felt. Deciding to go to the town square and sit there for a while, he headed down the main drag.

Mr. Brown passed Miss Marcy Adams with her black dog and Hunter Shaw with his latest rifle. Everyone looked so happy except for him. Then he stopped short to see a fine old man dressed up in a suit, accompanied by a lady in a long black dress. It was unlikely to see such fine folk dressed up in these parts, but they were probably heading back to Smithy after a day out in the boonies. Sure enough, they spotted the carriage that Mr. Brown had recently vacated and began walking toward it.

Watching for several minutes until the carriage disappeared in a great cloud of dust, Mr. Brown began unknowingly stomping the ground all around him from all the frustration that he felt.

"Why so glum, Mr. Brown?" called out a voice.

Mr. Brown looked up to see a fellow known as Trapper Jones. He was a tall, tough man with a great black beard and resembled a grizzly bear in many ways. The fellow sat upon a nearby wood pile, scraping down a couple of rabbit skins. Mr. Brown was not necessarily keen on Jones and his lifestyle, but all of a sudden, he felt sudden relief.

"I'll tell you what's the matter!" he said, venting his frustration by taking off his hat and smacking it against his leg. "We have a blasted sheriff in these parts who won't help an honest fellow!"

Jones gave a grunt of displeasure. "I coulda told you not to go to one of those law dogs!" He switched his knives and began on another skin. "And anyways, what didja you need?"

Mr. Brown came closer to the trapper and spoke in a more confidential tone. "A thief broke into my house this morning and ran off. I went to the sheriff's office in Smithy but Willikers said he was too busy on the Lawson's case."

Jones nodded a bit as he listened and then he looked up slowly from his work. "You ever see Trapper Jones at work?" he asked proudly, pointing his knife in Brown's direction. "I could track a squirrel that's been through the woods five days ago, and shoot it within an hour."

Brown was greatly impressed. "That sounds mighty good to me!"

"I could help you catch that thief," Jones said craftily, and then added, "for only a small fee."

"Well, it's a deal," Brown agreed, deciding that such a fee would indeed be small for such a great reward of having a thief brought to justice. Putting on his hat, he stuck out his hand as Jones rose to his feet.

Jones shook Brown's hand firmly and then said, "Meet me here tomorrow morning."

Brown nodded in agreement and turned to go with gladness in his heart. He knew that his wife did not like Jones, even less than he did, but at last, he felt that the matter could be properly taken care of. With that, he headed for home with a happy heart and a lightened step.

Meanwhile, after the trip to Shabby's and a nearby grocer's also in Wolf Den, Robert returned to the shack up on the hill, tired from his own trip. Having eaten along the way, he thought about a nice nap and trudged up to peek in at Pete, who was still sleeping. Tossing the boot down beside the sleeping man, he expected his partner to wake up, but he did not.

Bending over to make sure that Pete was all right, Robert noticed that there was a curious piece of paper in Pete's nearest hand. Reaching out carefully, Robert slipped the paper away and unfolded it, glancing over the rough map. Feeling a bit surprised at the sudden discovery, Robert immediately felt suspicious, wondering why it was that his partner had not told him about the treasure map.

Deciding to think the best about his friend, and to wait and see if Pete was saving it as a surprise, Robert carefully leaned over and stuck the map back in Pete's hand. Then he spent a couple of minutes unpacking the food. The noise finally caused Pete to stir.

Pete rolled over slightly but then realized that his friend was back and sat bolt upright in horror, immediately hiding the map from view.

"You're back!" Pete said in an angered panic. "Why didn't you tell me?"

"I tried to wake you up," Robert said in a genial tone.

"Oh," Pete said, relaxing and seeing his new boot nearby. "Good," he said, grabbing it and pulling it on. "But you've been gone way too short. I'm going back to sleep."

"It's only 7 o'clock," Robert said in surprise. "In the evening!"

Pete shrugged and rolled over, going back to sleep. With that, Robert decided that there was nothing left for him to do but go to sleep as well. Leaving the newly purchased goods lying sprawled around, he spread out his blanket and lay down for the night.

Early the next morning, when the stars were still shining and the moon hung in the treetops, Pete woke silently and carefully, looking all around him. Robert lay right beside him—fast asleep. Sitting up quietly, Pete reached for his hat and picked up the gun not too far from him. Creeping out of the shack, he began to collect the best of the gear, including the food and blankets that Robert had just bought, plus their shared frying pan, tin cup, and shovel.

After tying everything up into a neat sack and putting it around his shoulders, Pete headed for the deeper part of the woods beyond them. Pausing on the last part of the clearing, he glanced back at the shack and thought briefly of Robert.

"Bye, old boy," he said in a whisper. "My new friend? Gold Maps!"

With that, Pete left without another glance behind. He headed further up the hill as the dawn began to slowly break to reveal a cold and frosty morning. Trudging on and on through the dark woods into a great patch of hills and meadows beyond, Pete began to shiver uncontrollably from the cold.

It was early dawn and a prime time for travel, but Pete was exhausted. Stumbling on over a knoll, he rolled down into a patch of bushes that had just begun to bud, wrapped himself up in one of the blankets, and soon fell into an exhausted sleep.

It was now shortly after 6:00 AM. Robert woke up slowly to the sound of a gentle spring rain pattering all around him. Sitting up, he rubbed his patched face and said to his sleeping companion, "Come on, Pete, we gotta get up now."

Hearing no reply, Robert looked all around the shack, and then outside, but discovered that Pete was gone! Not only that but most of their gear was gone as well!

"That yellow-bellied skunk!" Robert screamed, shaking with anger. Furiously, he grabbed his hat and smashed it on his head, scrambling to his feet and rushing out of the shack with only his gray blanket and a sturdy stick. Another blanket lay nearby and a coil of rope hung on the side of the shack, so he seized both of those things and made off through the woods as fast as he could.

Not too long afterward, Pete woke up in the middle of a patch of thorn bushes, uncovering his head slowly from his own blanket and peeking from beneath his trusty hat. Realizing that it was raining, he groaned and immediately covered himself back up, but then he remembered his mission and struggled to get up in sudden excitement and desperation.

"I better be on the move!" he said to himself, hurrying to rise and pack his belongings. Realizing that he slept in too late and had no time for breakfast, Pete looked up in disgust at the rain coming down from the gray sky. It took only a moment longer for him to saddle himself up and then Pete was headed off across the nearest meadows. The map led him far across the hills in the remote part of Adamsville and the trail dipped down into the paths of the Rocky Mountain.

So, Pete trudged on and on that morning, through the bitter wind and damp cold, wishing all the while that he could be in a nice warm and dry spot, or at least have a horse to carry him and all of his gear through the slopes. As he came to the top of one fine hill, he could see all the newly grown buds and grasses sprouting all around him. Despite the bad weather and the cold, he felt his spirits beginning to lift just a little.

Pete smiled to himself as he enjoyed the fantastic scenery. "When I get that gold," he said to himself quietly, "I'm going to build a house here." Then he remembered his friend and laughed in an evil tone. "As for Robert, he can stay in that shack for all I care!"

Unbeknownst to Pete, however, Robert was not far behind! Peeking out from behind a bush along the nearest line of trees, Robert grinned nastily to see Pete standing at the top of the hill.

"Revenge," he breathed savagely, thinking with relish of how fortunate it was that he got a close glance at the Gold Maps and knew exactly where his unfaithful companion was headed. Watching as Pete stumbled on across the top of the hill, he thought for a second and then made a quick decision.

Turning to run directly down the slope parallel to the path that Pete was taking, he named the new trail his "shortcut to vengeance," and soon found himself on the outer ridge of the Rocky Mountain Pass. This informal road led down into a gully and somewhere beyond that lay another area that he needed to go through before finding the spot of the treasure, but he could not remember the rest of the directions. Knowing that Pete would soon be along, however, Robert tossed his blanket down and spent a few moments tossing his rope up in the branches of a sturdy tree and then hauling himself up to perch in a precarious place that overlooked the whole bank.

Not too long after, Pete came struggling down the pass with all of his gear and then paused, noticing a gray blanket lying across a branch on the side of the path. Thinking that it looked very much like Robert's blanket, Pete stared at it and then poked at it with the muzzle of his gun.

"But it can't be!" he muttered to himself in great confusion. "He's miles away!" Stumbling further down the path and looking in all directions, Pete heard a noise above him and looked up with horror to see Robert swinging down on a rope just behind him.

"Geronimo!" Robert cried out in glee.

Pete yelled in terror, but threw himself to the side and narrowly escaped being trampled on by Robert's muddy boots.

At that, it was Pete's turn to feel giddy. "Ha, you thought that was gonna work!" Then he eyed his partner in suspicion. "How did you find where I was?"

"I actually came for this," Robert replied, stepping forward and grabbing a precious piece of paper out of Pete's hand.

"No! My Gold Maps!" Pete cried in horror, but his dismay soon greatly increased when Robert followed up his trickery by giving Pete a shove that sent him falling down over the edge of the bank and into the muddy ravine below.

Robert watched Pete's descent with an evil laugh, calling down, "So long, fellow!" Then he quickly disappeared from sight.

At the bottom of the muddy ravine, Pete landed in a heap of old leaves and sticks. "He will pay for this," he said furiously, clenching his fists. He was happy to be safe and alive after the fall but was not at all looking forward to the ascent back up the cliff.

Several hours later, Pete finally hauled himself and his heavy pack over the last part of the cliff and back onto the sturdy part of Rocky Mountain Road. He sat there for some time, looking all around at his sorry plight and feeling quite despondent.

"All hope is lost," he said in despair. "I shall never be a rich man."

Then, suddenly, Pete remembered something and sat up straight with the realization. "All hope is not lost!" he told himself cheerfully. "My father always said, 'You don't give up 'til you're licked.' And I ain't licked!"

Rubbing the mud off his face, Pete grinned and pulled his shovel from his provisions. "Robert doesn't have a shovel. He can't dig!" Pulling open his sack of food, he opened it, saying, "Robert doesn't have food. He can't eat!"

Hungrily, Pete pulled out a hunk of bread and began munching on it ravenously. Then he pulled out a fine bottle and took an easy swig, enjoying the sudden bounty. In his haste to eat, however, he gave himself a sudden stomachache and simultaneously felt that he had no time to indulge in feasting. Impatiently, he tossed away the bread in frustration. Then he went to pick up the bottle but accidentally knocked it over instead and, when he took another swig, he realized that dropping it had caused mud to get jammed in the stem. So, he resorted to spitting and sputtering until the mud was out of his mouth. Forcing himself to remain solemn, Pete set the cork back in the bottle, put it away in his sack, and loaded himself up until he looked more like a misshapen pack mule than a human being.

"I better be off," he said as he finally took off again, remembering which was the way the map directed him to go. Carefully making his way around the muddy spots and protruding stones and roots, Pete followed the pass all the way to the end of a gully. To lift his spirits from the next journey ahead, he said aloud, "Here I come, Robert!" and continued on unabated.

Not too long after, Robert finally found the field that the map directed him to cross. He had wasted far too long backtracking his steps after taking a wrong turn down Rocky Mountain Road, but he was finally back to the right spot.

Pushing his hat off of his forehead for a second on the edge of the field he had just walked across, Robert glanced around. He looked up at the sky and thought, "Good, that blasted rain stopped!" Then he began to trudge along the edge of the woods, wondering about the stream that the map directed him to follow next. Not too long after, he went over a small knoll and found a little trickle of water running into a gully that eventually ran into the Lone Pine Stream. Happily, he went down, slipping and sliding and nearly falling into the gully several times, but not too much time elapsed before he came to a great big rock marked with an X.

Delighted, Robert stood upon the rock and looked at his map again. Checking off the places that he had already gone, he read the next part aloud.

"Go east, eight large steps from a rock marked with an X. There stands a tree with the treasure buried beneath."

Robert tapped the rock with his boot and studied the sky before turning slightly toward the east and counting as he walked eight large steps. When he came to a stop, he glanced around with a bit of bewilderment. There was no tree in sight, but only a rotted stump half-buried in leaves.

"Where's the tree?" he wondered, glancing around. Then he suddenly put it all together. "Oh! Here's the stump," he realized, and then turned slightly to see a fallen tree beside him, "and there's the tree!" He stood there for a moment, studying the map, and then turned back to the stump.

"Now to dig," he declared with great relish and delight, putting away the map. Just then, a horrible realization struck him. "Cringo!" he swore aloud. "I forgot a shovel!"

Just that moment, a shovel came down, and "Clunk!" hit him on top of the head.

"Ooh!" cried Robert and immediately fell down.

It was Pete! "You won't be needing a shovel!" he said with an evil laugh, looking at his prone friend and tossing aside his gun and blanket so that he could do the digging.

Happily, Pete stuck the shovel into the ground by the rotted stump and began to dig. After just a few stabs, however, he hit something solid. He was inclined to be delighted, but Pete suddenly felt suspicious.

"Why's it so close to the surface? That's funny." Setting aside the shovel, he got down on the ground and clawed the loose dirt aside in a few short seconds.

Pulling out a chest wrapped in a dirty sheet, Pete set the chest down and unlatched it, his hopes and dreams about to be revealed.

"Ahh!" Robert suddenly yelled, having recovered from the blow to his head and throwing himself on Pete like a madman.

The two fellows scuffled a bit and then Pete managed to shove the smaller man aside so he could finally throw the chest open. It was empty!

Both Pete and Robert gaped down into the chest and found a note. Reading it in unison, they said, "Found! Fall 1858."

Pete threw himself away from the chest in disgust. "That was last fall!" he said in great disappointment.

Robert was likewise infuriated, but so much so that he was speechless.

At that very moment, a small log rolled down the hill toward them and almost hit Pete.

"Where did that come from?" wondered Robert, getting to his feet to investigate.

"I don't know," Pete said, just as surprised. Rising as well, he began going up the hill, unable to see very far up but hearing something rustling in the leaves somewhere above them. "What's that sound?" he asked.

At the top of the hill, Mr. Brown was recovering from tripping on a nearby log. "Trapper!" he yelled. "Someone went this way!"

Trapper Jones was at his side in a few quick bounds. "You're making more noise than a herd of elephants!" he said with frustration and anger. "Why are you on the ground? Get up!"

Accepting the hand that Jones extended to him, Brown rose quickly, brushing off his knees. "I tripped over a log." Picking up his gun that he had dropped a couple of feet away, he looked pointedly at Jones. "Anyhow, what were you doing? Someone plainly went this way."

"There must be two of them, then," Jones explained, noting the boot marks on the ground. "I saw some tracks near the riverbed." He began following the tracks that led to the edge of the knoll.

Brown also began to resume his search, but he looked further away than Jones and quickly spotted Robert and Pete standing at the bottom of the hill.

"There they are!" he shouted in great excitement, far too loud for Jones, who immediately snapped upright.

"Quiet!" said the trapper a bit peevishly, but then he caught sight of the two fellows staring up at them. "There *are* two of them!" he said, his blood beginning to boil. "Come on!" With a swift motion, he jerked for Brown to follow him and they began running diagonally down the hill.

At the bottom of the hill, Robert and Pete appeared shocked and terrified.

"It's the man you stole from," said Robert, recognizing the shorter man. "Mr. Brown!"

"And Trapper Jones!" Pete added, beginning to tremble with fear. He looked all around in dismay and then grabbed his hat, hoping that he could beat the two men to the stream. "Let's get out of here!" he said to Robert, seeing that the younger man was picking up the gun.

Instead of following him, however, Robert said, "I'll handle this!" and pointed the gun straight up the hill toward their descending pursuers.

"No!" Pete cried out, rushing back to his friend and grabbing his arm. "You haven't met Jones!"

"I can take care of ruffians!" Robert replied with a gleeful grin, unabated.

"No!" Pete repeated, beginning to visibly tremble with fear. Seeing that he was unable to stop Robert, he turned and dashed off through the woods.

Undeterred, Robert shot the gun—but missed cleanly. Seeing the two men come to a quick halt and the bear-like fellow raise his own gun, he immediately dropped the rifle and dashed away, his hand on his hat to keep it from flying off.

"So! You think you know how to shoot!" Jones said in anger and indignation. He stood halfway down the hill with Mr. Brown not far behind. Throwing down his axe and pointing his own gun straight down at the fleeing thieves with one arm extended, he paused to glance at Brown.

"You want them dead or alive?"

Brown hesitated and then said in a genial tone, "They haven't done anything deserving of death. So, keep them alive."

Jones appeared a bit skeptical towards Brown's niceties, but all he said was, "Come on!" and they continued in their descent to the bottom of the hill.

Pete and Robert rushed through the woods as fast as they could go.

Robert was beginning to feel out of breath but managed to call out to his friend just ahead, "Where are you bringing us?"

Just that moment, Pete put on the brakes and whirled about, beginning to uncover a small tub that had been hidden by a pile of sticks and leaves.

"Help me, if you will!" Pete said, tossing an armful to Robert, who tossed it aside and leaned in to help lift the tub from its place on the forest floor.

They carried it hastily to the nearby riverside and Robert wondered at this new marvel that his friend had uncovered for the afternoon.

"What is this?" he finally asked, as they marched through the tall grasses and to the edge of the Lone Pine Stream.

Nearly out of breath, Pete replied, "My father always said, 'Never get caught without a way of escape.' Put it down, my fellow."

At that, they flipped the tub over and Pete shoved it into the stream, instructing Robert to hold onto the side as he grabbed the supplies and two poles, tossing them into the tub. Handing Robert a pole, he said, "Come on!" and leaped inside.

"Whoa," Robert said nervously as he climbed in after Pete, clearly not used to being in the boat. As he watched Pete expertly use the poles to distance their tub from the shore, he wondered, "What is this rum bathtub anyway?"

"Tub! Tub!" Pete cried out, deeply offended by the casual reference. "You should be thanking me! I made this with my own hands!"

Then the two men poled away, out of sight from where they cast off.

Back on the riverbank, Jones rushed up to a fallen log and gazed out at the quickly escaping men. Sinking his axe into the log and resting his boot nearby, he glanced back and waited for Brown to catch up to him.

"It will be a bit more difficult in catching them now," Jones told Brown when he struggled up, nearly out of breath. "In half an hour, I'll have a boat ready."

Brown shrugged at that, already having spent enough time and energy on the matter to be further concerned. "It isn't worth the trouble," he told the trapper. "They didn't steal anything, anyways."

Jones's temper immediately flared. "You didn't tell me that part before!" Seeing the smaller man's careless shrug, the trapper turned from the river. "Well, if that's the case, let's be off."

Agreeably, Brown turned from Jones, heading back through the woods as he began to think about his next duties for the day. Before he got too far away from the trapper, the rich man heard Jones shout after him.

"And what about my pay?"

"Oh, yeah, yeah," said Brown dismissively, not at all unfamiliar with people's constant demand for his money.

Pete and Robert continued to struggle along down the Lone Pine Stream as it began to pick up pace and head toward the rapids.

Robert began to feel nervous, thinking about the rapids and falls that they would need to get through before entering the calmer waters connecting them to the Running River. "Do you even know anything about handling a boat in a river?" he wondered, attempting to sound bold.

"River?" scoffed Pete. "This is a puddle to me!"

"Puddle?" replied Robert, handling his pole with even more fear and dread. "I wouldn't be too sure about that!"

"What?" shouted Pete, the sound of the water now becoming too loud for normal conversation.

Robert gave up trying to explain, focusing all his attention on trying to help his friend as they navigated the rapids of the stream. He felt a bit sick as the tub tossed and turned, despite Pete's expert skills, and managed to drop his pole, needing to hold on for dear life instead.

Miles downstream, a young lad sat on the bank of the stream with his fishing pole. He and his father lived out in the sticks of Chief's Run with his mother and five little sisters. For months, he had looked forward to a day off from regular farm work to go fishing with his father, but now that the day had come, it had been one disaster after another.

First, their chickens had found all the worms he had saved and ate them all up, hardly leaving a scrap for a hungry fish. Then, his two sisters had hidden his pole, and when he had finally found it, he discovered that one of their cows had trampled on it and snapped it in half. So he had to borrow his father's ratty old spare pole. If that wasn't the worst yet, his father had tried his best to make the day special for him, but the farmer was such a cranky and cantankerous fellow himself that Eddie despaired of the whole day. And true to form, after finally managing to find a couple of grubby worms in the bank near the river, nothing had bit, not even the tiniest minnow. His father had stepped away for a smoke and then came back, telling him that they would try a bit further downstream, but Eddie simply sat there, refusing to move.

Eddie's father came back from his smoke break with his fish trap and pole in hand and sat down. Immediately, he pointed upstream to a great tub approaching them. Father and son gazed at the empty tub as it floated by lazily and headed around a bend in the stream.

As it grew smaller and smaller from sight, the lad stuck out his lower lip. "No fish? No care," Eddie said despondently.

"Yah," his father replied, nodding in agreement. They both continued to stare at the tub as it vanished from sight, completely failing to see a black hat floating by in the wake of the tub.

What had happened to Pete and Robert? Would anyone discover the truth of what had taken place in the deserted tub before it reached the hick father and his disappointed son?

To be continued...

3
The Sheriff's Discovery

Tales from Buck's County, Part II

One fine morning in the sprawling countryside of Buck's County, Sheriff Tom Hutchinson of the Village of Smithy sat in his office, reading the newspaper and drinking his morning coffee. He slowly took a swig and turned the page to look at the section about law and order.

"'Pon my word," he said in surprise, sitting up straight and setting his mug down with a plunk. He stared down at the page and then shook his head. "Things are bad next door."

Life was challenging out west when sheriffs had a hard time maintaining order and were generally disrespected as "scurvy law dogs" by the numerous ruffians that ran wild. Sheriff Tom well knew that the job of protecting the people was difficult since he had been in the business for nearly ten years now. But now that he had just arrived in town last month from the county seat of

Quentin to try and straighten things out, he had been finding this task to be even more challenging as time went on.

It did not help that many country sheriffs ruined their own reputations and people were generally distrustful of those who were supposed to be the most trustworthy of all citizens. The previous sheriff of Smithy and its surrounding towns only did what he wanted and took extra money from the poor townsfolk. That selfish man had been dismissed by the Marshall over three years ago, but his deputy, an older man named Steve Willikers, was tired and overworked after trying to keep the area in order on his own. Most of Deputy Steve's duties involved settling land squabbles, chasing mad dogs, and finding runaway horses. Unfortunately, that meant that when real trouble with robbers and bandits arose, the people often found his help to be lacking because he was so tired from all the petty problems they brought to him on a regular basis.

As he thought about all of that, Sheriff Tom looked at the paper again and read the headline slowly.

"City of Garbey in Disarray," the paper claimed, and had a whole half-page to prove it. There was even a blurry picture of a bearded man with the caption, "Robbers Run Wild All Day and Night."

"Garbey is only a hunrit miles from here," Hutchinson mused to himself, looking at the map hanging on the wall and scratching his head in thought. To the average farmer or trapper from

Adamsville, Chief's Run, Coatestown, or Bob's Mill, it was too far away to worry about danger from the big city.

But the new sheriff disagreed. "A hunrit miles only gives a dangerous thief extry time to think up a hunrit new mischiefs to do in a small defenseless town."

Sheriff Hutchinson thought seriously as he rose from his desk, swiping his hat from the nearby rack and placing it on his head. Then he fastened on his gun belt and holster and headed for the door.

He opened the door and stood there, looking out into the bright morning and the quiet streets of the little village. "Buck's County ain't defenseless," he said determinedly. "No siree, not this time." With that, the stocky little man smiled and patted his gun belt as he headed out to bravely face the day and all the troubles it might hold.

That same morning, Farmer Jackson sat on his porch in Coatestown, trying to fix his plow. His faithful dog Trevor sat nearby, soaking in the morning sun. Then the house door opened and his wife stepped out onto the porch. She looked at her husband curiously.

"What happened, Bobby?" she asked, coming to stand beside him.

He sighed and shook his head. "Another repair to do," he said in regret. "With too much rain, this ground is too soft and the plow ain't working right. Poor ox can't plow with the mud so thick, and I can't plant more wheat. And when—"

"I know all about farming, dear," Sally said a bit spitefully as she interrupted him. "What about those parts the hardware store in Wolf Den sold you?"

Jackson snorted in derision. "That good-for-nothing Jeff Shabby!" He threw down his piece of plow, watching it clank onto the stones at the bottom of the steps. "I'll have to go to the city to buy something of quality. There ain't a metal worker worth his beans in the whole countryside."

"The city! You don't mean Garbey! That's a hundred miles away!" Sally objected. "Think of all the time you'll waste going way down there. Surely there's someone in Smithy who can help you out!"

"Naw, I've looked and I've tried," Jackson said. "Believe me, it's not worth it. I'd have better success starting my own metal working business than trade with those lazy bones that try to call themselves smithies." He stood up and shrugged in resignation. "I have no choice. I'm going to Garbey, and maybe I'll hire a personal metalworker on my way back."

Then he smiled at Sally, and then at the dog. "But don't you worry. I'll be back in no time and I'll have Trapper Jones keep an eye on things for me."

"That piece of filth!" Sally shuddered in disgust, remembering how grubby he was. "You'll have to pay him a pretty penny to get to help with anything, and that's a pretty penny that we don't have!"

"Well, he is a hard worker," Jackson replied after some thought. "Anyway, he minds his own business and doesn't cause any trouble, even if he is an odd character. But he won't rob us blind like some others might."

"All right, well, I'll pack you up some food and supplies," Sally said, turning to the door. "Will you go by wagon or coach?"

Jackson brushed the dirt from his knees and turned to pick up his broken metal parts. "Stagecoach. I'll get Murphy to give me a deal. He will, I'm sure. He always does." He smiled as he turned to call the dog to come with him back to the barn.

Within the hour, Farmer Jackson was on his way down to Smithy to catch the stagecoach into Garbey. He strolled into the village, remembering how he had wasted his time at Shabby's just a few weeks ago, and ended up buying several things that the man practically forced on him, things that he did not need and things that his wife certainly did not want cluttering up the small property they lived on.

Sighing, he nearly bumped into Deputy Steve as he reached Smithy. Touching his hat, he nodded to the older man and then headed over to the office to talk to Murphy about the best price to head down to the city with as short a trip as possible. The negotiations were short and successful, and he was soon on his way.

Back at the farm that evening, Sally walked out on the porch to make sure the animals had what they needed for the night. She had just about finished and was bringing in the eggs from the chickens when she suddenly stopped, seeing Trapper Jones walking out from the edge of the woods. Recoiling, she quickly went up the stairs and disappeared inside the house, slamming and locking the door.

She muttered to herself as she hid in the next room and peered out the window. "Ugh! That grubby man! He just eats and eats and smells like a bear! He looks like a bear, too! I won't have anything to do with him!"

Trapper Jones, not realizing that his presence was so unwelcome, walked up to the door and knocked. Not hearing a reply, he shrugged and turned away, deciding to chop some wood and fry up a mess of squirrels before turning in for the night.

The next morning, Sally stepped outside early to feed the chickens and immediately spotted a tired-looking young man sitting next to the wood pile with their dog quietly resting beside him.

"Why, hello," she said in surprise, going up to him. "Did you chop all this wood?"

"Well, ma'am—" he began nervously, appearing rather awkward as he stood up and fumbled with his hat that had been resting upon his knee. "I just—"

"You poor boy, you must be all tired out!" Sally said, cutting him off since she had heard quite enough, "Come along, I need to feed the chickens, and then I will fix you up a fine breakfast, and how about some chamomile tea? You do look rather ill, my poor lad."

"Thank you, ma'am," the man stammered, still obviously embarrassed. "I—I'll be fine."

"No, no, I do insist! Now come along," she replied, taking charge of the situation. As they crossed the yard to the chicken pen, she noticed how nervous he looked as he peered all around, as if he was afraid of something.

"What is your name, sonny?" she asked, looking up at him curiously.

"I—um—well, my name's Jim," he finally said. "Trapper Jim. I—I'm not really from around here."

"I can see that," she said kindly, tossing out the grain for the chickens. "Now, run along, girls, and lay me some eggs!" she called after them and turned back to find Jim looking as if he would immediately run away.

"Now don't be scared, sonny," she said, patting his arm and motioning him back to the house. "Come along, and I'll make you a fine hearty breakfast. How about flapjacks? With real syrup? And some fried eggs on the side to give you some strength, and some goodly sausages?" Seeing that he began to look interested in the mention of food, she smiled and tugged on his arm. "Well, come along, then, right into the farmhouse with you, and get you all washed up, too. Were you sleeping in the mud?"

Before he had a chance to answer or to look too embarrassed, Jim found himself in the house, right in front of a clean basin of water and a plush towel.

"Here you go, sonny," she said. "Wash up, and let me put breakfast on the table!"

Jim stared into the water as she disappeared and then soberly began to wash his face and hands. The water was not too hot, so he found it quite nice after a minute, and he began to wonder if he needed a whole bath.

"No, I don't got time for a bath," he said to his reflection that was shimmering with splashes and looking rather grubby. "I need to get some good food, and then be on my way." With that, he dried off his face and hands quickly, smoothed down his hair in the looking glass, and then walked into the kitchen to see a great big stack of flapjacks awaiting his hungry belly.

As he ate, Sally sat down in her rocking chair with her knitting and began to talk to him, asking him questions that he could not answer because his mouth was full, and instead telling him all about the farm, the cows, the chickens, her husband's broken plow, the dog, and how nasty Trapper Jones smelled.

"Trapper Jones?" Jim said, his eyes bulging as he spoke nervously with his mouth full. "Is he around here?"

Sally cackled a bit and shook her knitting needle at him. "Never you worry, sonny boy! Our good dog will keep him far away! Jones, that old rascal, knows that he is no match for Trevor, and one bark from Trevor keeps him far away. Funny thing, though, Jones only comes after Trevor comes inside the house with me, doesn't he?" she said, looking down at the dog as he sat on the rug, smiling up at his mistress.

Jim listened with round eyes as he continued to eat. The food was good, but the poor young man was so nervous he did not know what to think. But soon, breakfast was done, and he was feeling much better.

"Thank you kindly, ma'am," he said in a genuine tone, picking up his hat. "It hit the spot. As my father always said, 'Best food is a home-cooked meal by a farmer's wife'."

"Well, that's fine, just fine," Sally said with a giggle. "But come along, now, let me show you around, and I'll make you a nice little spot in the barn to stay until you get some rest, and grow some meat on those bones!"

It only took Sally a few minutes to show Jim around the small farm and then she gave him a clean blanket and told him to make himself a nice bed when he was tired.

"You just make yourself comfortable here, and don't worry about a thing," she told him, heading back to the house. Then she called back, "There's a good pitchfork in the barn, and the cow pen needs cleaned out, and I have some more mending to do. But lunch will be at noon, and it will be waiting for you!"

With that, she called to the dog to make sure he would stay on the porch and then disappeared back into the house.

Jim stood there for a moment, looking at the pitchfork hanging on the wall, then out the door at the cow way down in the pasture, and then at the nice clean straw bed. Smiling to himself, he took the fork from his back pocket that he had swiped from the breakfast table and picked his teeth for a moment. Then he fluffed up the cozy blanket and lay down for a comfortable nap.

Several hours later, Jim awoke with a start. "Oh no, it's nearly noon, and I didn't do any work for that old farm lady!" Jumping to his feet, he stumbled over to grab the pitchfork, but just that moment, Mrs. Jackson and the dog came walking into the barn.

"Why, there you are!" she said in surprise. "Lunchtime came and went, and I called and rang the dinner bell, but no reply! What happened?"

Jim stumbled about awkwardly, but then caught sight of a fishing pole nearby and blurted out, "I—I went fishing! I wanted to catch you a nice fish for dinner, but lost track of time and forgot about the cow pen and—"

Sally's laughter interrupted him. "Why, you poor silly boy. Well, you can catch me a fish another day. I am going into town to buy some goods. Why don't you come with me? You can look around for a job, I reckon, since I think you have a better head on you than for trapping and fishing, and even farming. Have you ever thought about working for the general store? Or how about the bank?"

Jim seemed mesmerized by the mention of possibly working for the bank and obediently helped her out as she set up the wagon for an excursion to town.

Not too long afterward, they reached Smithy. "Now, I need to make some purchases but feel free to look around. I'll be back presently, but if you can't find me, I'll probably be in Mrs. Davenport's shop looking at her goods."

"Yes, ma'am," Jim said quietly, holding onto the reins and waiting until she was out of sight. Then he quickly got down, tied up the reins, and went down the street to look at the bank.

Sheriff Tom walked around the corner to head back to his office when he saw an unfamiliar young man suddenly stop in the middle of the street, jump a couple of feet in the other direction, and then run down the nearest alley. Surprised, Tom ran after him, but when he looked around the corner, the young man in the white hat was nowhere to be seen.

"Curious thing," he muttered to himself, and then quickly turned and trotted down to his office, finding Steve at the desk.

"Quick, Steve! You're the fastest typist around here! I need to send out a letter to the Marshall, quick as a jackrabbit!"

Steve looked up from his paperwork, rather surprised, but quickly put a piece of paper in the machine and began to type at the sheriff's direction.

"Address it to the Marshall of the City of Quentin, Buck's County."

"Of course," Steve said, a bit puzzled by the formality. "Now what?"

"Are you ready?" Tom demanded.

"Yes," Steve slowly said, becoming more and more puzzled.

"Then type fast! Here we are: Dear Sir!" Sheriff Tom began. "It has come to my attention that the City of Garbey is being overrun by mobsters, bandits, and ruffians of all types and occupations. Please send me at once a list of the county's most dangerous criminals, so that I can hereby remain on the lookout for any nefarious persons that would cause harm to my good townsfolk in the Village of Smithy and all surrounding regions.

"I am particularly concerned about any ruffians who may be hiding in the Lone Pine District and waiting for the perfect opportunity to escape from the forests and strike our fine village and towns with looting, raiding, and all sorts and manners of evil. I will wait for your reply as soon as you are able to send it, and I send you my good will and a hearty handshake.

"Greetings and well-wishes on all your family, Thomas Hutchinson, Sheriff of the Village of Smithy."

After quickly typing out the last sentence, Steve sat back, scratched his head, and laughed. "He knows who you are, Tom, you worked right next to him for eight years."

"Never mind that!" Tom said in a blustery tone, beginning to look embarrassed but waving the remark off. "Run it off to the telegraph office and wait there for a reply, my good man. The Marshall is a fine fellow, and he will get back to me as soon as he hears my request."

Steve took out the paper with a flourish, handed it to Tom so he could look it over, and then left the office as quickly as he could put on his hat. As he left, he shook his head slightly.

"Always a one for show, that Tom. He should have been a war general instead of a sheriff!" Then he stopped and laughed. "Or maybe he just likes the sound of the typewriter?" Shaking his head again, he went on to pass the message to the telegraph office.

Meanwhile, Sheriff Tom stood by the window and took a minute to compose himself. Taking a deep breath, he quietly left the office to go over to the dry goods store. He stood outside by the window, looking around and thinking for a minute, when someone called him.

"Why, hello, Mrs. Jackson," he said calmly as the older lady came up to him to take his hand. He made a little bow and took off his hat. "How is everything on the farm, ma'am?"

"Fine, just fine!" she said, quite happy to talk. "Everything is very good, though I wish Bobby would hurry up and come back soon. It is a shame that we don't have a good blacksmith anywhere around here, and I do wish one would move to the area! But it is all right. I will tell you, though," she went on, "a wonderful thing happened today!"

"What was that?" he wondered as he placed his hat back on his head and offered her his arm to help her back to the wagon.

"A young man named Trapper Jim came by to help me out!" she said, very happily. "It is such a relief to have him around instead of that nasty bear of a character, Trapper Jones!"

Sheriff Tom laughed a bit. "Trapper Jones is a bit of a bear, but he is completely harmless, ma'am."

"Well, that is what everyone says, but I do not care. I say that cleanliness is next to godliness, and there is no way that man is a fine fellow when he smells like a sack of wet dogs!"

Although the sheriff seemed about to say something else, she went right on without giving him a chance to speak.

"But never mind that, I do not mean to complain! I will tell you, though, that this young fellow is such a blessing out of heaven, an angel in disguise! He is polite, even though he is a bit shy and very nervous, and he is the sweetest thing. He even wanted to catch me a fish for dinner, but I don't know how good he is at that sort of thing. In fact, I wouldn't tell just anyone this," she added, lowering her voice, "but I am a bit worried about him because he seems a bit sickly and tired all the time. He said he went fishing, but I think he slept all day."

"Perhaps he is not tired, perhaps he is lazy," Tom suggested.

"Perhaps, but I think something terrible must have happened to him for him to be so nervous around regular honest people!" She seemed about to say more, but then she stopped and pointed. "Oh! There he is. Jim! Trapper Jim!"

The young man in the white hat stood not too far away and turned slowly, appearing very nervous as he obediently walked up to Mrs. Jackson and the sheriff. He took off his hat, trembling a bit.

"Why, it's you!" Sheriff Tom said in surprise, looking at the young man. "Why did you run away from me before? Did you steal anything, son?"

"No, sir, I'm sorry, sir, Sheriff, sir," Jim said, fumbling with his hat. "You see, I was nervous, hearing stories about law dogs from Trapper Jones, you know, and, well, as my father always said, 'You have to trust a man as far as you can throw him,' and I'm not very good at throwing people, sir."

At that, the sheriff and Mrs. Jackson laughed. "Well, son, there's nothing to worry about," Sheriff Tom said, helping the lady up into the wagon. "You settle down at the farm, and when Farmer

Jackson returns, he'll make sure you have a fine job tossing hay and you won't need to worry about throwing people around."

"Good, sir, thank you, sir, that's fine, sir," Jim said nervously, getting up into the wagon beside Mrs. Jackson.

"Well," Tom began but then caught sight of Steve coming down the road. "I need to go. Goodbye, Mrs. Jackson! Goodbye, Jim!"

"Goodbye, goodbye," Mrs. Jackson called out, motioning for Jim to pick up the reins.

Sheriff Tom quickly followed Steve into the office. "Well, what's the good word from up in Quentin? Let me see that list, my good man."

Steve handed him the list and began to empty his pockets and take off his badge. "Afraid it's not much of anything," he said, yawning a bit and stretching. "And it's been a long day. How late are you working 'til? I'm heading off to supper and catch a game of checkers with Murphy. How'd you like to join us?"

Tom finally put down the paper with a sigh. "Well, I'm too busy, catching up on records and paperwork." He looked back at the paper with a bit of a frown and then turned to put his hat up on the rack. "You can have Johnny send me over some supper if you want. But I need to finish this up, before something big hits and I miss all the signs. It's a tough world out there, Steve, my good man."

"Suit yourself," Deputy Steve said quietly, heading off to the door. "See you tomorrow."

"Goodnight," Tom said, sitting down at the desk and reaching for a fat stack of papers. As the room slowly began to grow dark, he lit a match to a nearby candle and continued reading.

Another hour passed as Sheriff Tom continued to slowly read all of the records. His candle began to burn lower and lower, but suddenly, he sat up straight and rustled the papers in front of him. He stared at it and then got up, going to find another candle. After he lit it hurriedly, he sat down again and picked up the paper, beginning to read out loud.

"Mr. Brown came in today, complaining about a young man with a white hat, yellow hair, and a fork."

"A fork?" Tom wondered, staring at the paper closely. "The young man was trying to steal his gold watch and his gold ring but only got away with an old piece of paper that was useless to him. And then he took the guy's boot off during a fist fight!"

Tom laughed and got up, pacing around the room. "I remember Steve telling me some of the crazy things that happen in this village, but this is ridiculous!" He stopped by the window and looked out at the lantern from the tavern across the street. He listened, hearing Steve's voice in his head.

"You best be careful of Mr. Brown, he has a terrible temper, even though you wouldn't know it at first. He brought in the boot and the fork one day and almost hurled them in my face when I told him that I was too busy to go track down some kid that was up to nothing but mischief."

Shaking his head, Tom went into the back room and dug out a box, finding the boot and the fork and looking over them carefully. Finding nothing important, he returned to his desk and blew out one candle.

"Well, nothing here. I better get some sleep." Yawning, he picked up the candlestick and carried it into the back room where his cot was. He put down the candle and sat down to take off his boots. Soon enough, he blew out the candle, lay down on the cot, and fell asleep almost instantly.

Sheriff Tom awoke with some of the earliest birds when it was still pale outside. Rising, he put on his boots and went outside to wash his face and hands at the basin by the door. Shaking the water from his face, he stepped back inside and picked up his hat on the rack, then put on his gun belt, and walked down the road to get some breakfast at the inn.

After a hearty early breakfast, Tom headed over to Jackson's farm to check on Sally and to let her know that Murphy said the stage would be arriving later that night. When he arrived, he found Sally feeding the chickens and singing Trapper Jim's praises.

"Oh, he is simply wonderful to have around," she said when Tom asked how everything was going with Farmer Jackson still away.

"That is wonderful news indeed," Tom said. "Is he a good worker, ma'am?"

"Well," Sally admitted after a moment, "I am still a bit worried about him, Sheriff, since he sleeps so much and always looks so pale and sad. Do you think I should call round to Doc Benson?"

"Where is he now?" Sheriff Tom wondered, looking around the farm.

"Probably sleeping, poor lad," Sally said. "Would you mind checking in on him?"

"I would be glad to, ma'am," he replied, tipping his hat and beginning to walk toward the barn.

Sheriff Tom quietly slipped in through the big barn doors and stood there for a moment, allowing his eyes to adjust to the darkness. Seeing a hat resting on a nearby post, he walked around the corner to see the young man called Trapper Jim asleep in a pile of hay. His clothes were rather grubby as if they had not been changed or washed in many days, and even though he was asleep, he tossed and turned a bit, as if his mind was full of dreams.

"Robert!" he suddenly called out, and Sheriff Tom drew back, in case Jim woke up and saw him. But then Jim settled down and simply muttered, "Gold maps."

Tom took a step forward and peered down in the darkness, noticing that Jim's boots were different. He was not surprised but made a careful mental note, and wondered if he should tell Sally about his suspicion or simply wait until Bob returned home.

"Father!" Jim suddenly called out again. "Trapping comes to no good end," he mumbled and then rolled over, burying his head in his arms and sighing.

Sheriff Tom had heard enough. Tiptoeing out of the barn, he slipped back into the daylight and stood there for a minute, rubbing his eyes and thinking. Robert? He was not familiar with any trappers named Robert, so he decided to do some investigations before mentioning it to Farmer Jackson or his wife.

Just then, Tom heard the sound of wood being split. Going around the corner of the barn, he found Trapper Jones standing there, having just finished splitting a stack of logs for Mrs. Jackson. The sheriff grinned slightly and looked at the house, seeing the door close and knowing that the lady was probably hiding from the bearded trapper like she usually did.

Then Trapper Jones spotted Sheriff Tom and stood there, his thumbs stuck in his belt and a bit of a frown on his face.

"Hello, Jones," Tom said, stepping forward and extending his hand in greeting.

"Sheriff," Trapper Jones acknowledged in a surly tone, not moving a muscle to shake his hand.

Shrugging, the sheriff put down his hand and said in a casual tone, "Well, I know you don't like me much as an officer of the law, but I have nothing against you. In fact, I have a favor to ask you about an investigation since I know you know these parts better than anyone in a fifty-mile radius."

"That's true," Jones said, relaxing his stance and appearing a bit less cranky. "And I ain't got a problem with law dogs if you stick to your business and let me stick to mine."

"Which is just fine," Tom replied, "the world would be a much more peaceful place if everyone had that motto."

Jones nodded slightly, not caring for high talk and philosophy. "Well, what didja need?"

"Well, it's like this," Sheriff Tom said quietly, stepping forward a bit. "I don't want to worry Mrs. Jackson, but as you know, Bob is coming back tonight and there's a young fellow in the barn who seems to be ailing something poor, but I need to do some investigations on him. I just want you to keep a special eye on things, I'm not saying anything will happen or this fellow will be trouble because he seems rather ill to me, but better safe than sorry."

"Is that all?" Jones said, a bit insulted. "You want me to be nursemaid to some weasel of a kid?"

"No, sir, not at all," Tom said quickly. "I want you to make sure that Mrs. Jackson stays safe until tonight, and then if I need help with tracking, then I will let you know."

Jones still sounded surly. "Well, that silly old lady doesn't need any help, but I'm watching the place anyway for Jackson, that's what I'm here for."

"I appreciate it," the sheriff said, deciding to let the conversation drop there. "Have a good day, Jones." Tipping his hat, he turned and was about to walk away, but then he paused. "Jones?"

"What?" the man demanded, picking up his axe again.

"If anything suspicious happened this side of the District, would you be willing to tell me about it?"

"I might, but I might not," the trapper replied, neither angry nor kindly.

"I appreciate the honesty," Tom said, then nodded again and headed back to the village. On the way back, he thought long and hard about the situation and then decided that there was only one other person who could help him out.

Back at the farm, Jim woke up slowly and rolled over, groping for his hat. Seeing it hanging on the post above him, he rose, put it on his head, and then stumbled outside. Just beyond the door, he caught sight of the woodpile and froze. Then he looked beyond to see a man pitching out the cow pen.

"Trapper Jones!" he said in dismay, turning back to the barn. "I gotta get out of here!" He rushed around the barn, wondering if there was a good place to hide, but then found an old coat and put it on, picking up a pail and a fishing pole and deciding to go fishing.

"As my father always said, 'Make believe you're busy, and no one will suspect that you're running away'."

Before leaving for the woods, Jim carefully made his way to the farmhouse door, but when he knocked on the window, there was no reply.

"Goodbye, Mrs. Jackson," he finally said through the keyhole. "Thank you for your kindness."

With that, he took a quick glance around and then headed for the woods and the river beyond.

Sheriff Tom hurried into his office to find his deputy reading the paper. Steve immediately looked up with a guilty expression, shoved the paper into the nearby desk drawer, and then began typing furiously on the typewriter.

"Never mind, never mind," Tom said quickly, walking up to his gun cabinet and beginning to rummage around for extra bullets. "I just talked to Murphy who said the stage is on its way back by now, so Farmer Jackson should be home by nightfall. Good thing, too, since I have to ride on up to Adamsville for an investigation."

Steve stopped typing and looked up at Tom in wonder. "Adamsville? That will take you all day, and then half the night, too!"

"I need to talk to Mr. Brown about that incident with the fork and the boot."

Steve shook his head with a bit of worry. "You best be careful, son, he's a real hot head! In fact," he said, rising, "you best let me ride up there and take care of it for you. I know how to handle the fellow."

"Well, all right, but I want you to ask him particularly about the description of the young man that broke into his house some time ago. And ask him about the description of both the thieves that he had Trapper Jones track down for him."

As he watched Steve go to the door to put on his hat, he called after him, "Oh, and one more thing! Stop by Jeff Shabby's if you have time. He sends me a letter every week about some dimwit that only bought one boot, and he didn't care if it was a left or a right boot, and his spelling is dreadful! Make sure to buy that leftover boot that he kept complaining about so we can use it as evidence."

Deputy Steve stopped and looked back at Tom. "Did you find the thieves?"

"Well, I have a hunch that I found one, but methinks there is more to the story, and I'm bound to find out."

"All right, well, I will be back tomorrow bright and early, then," Steve said, opening the door and stepping out.

"Fine, just fine," Tom said, beginning to sit down at the desk, but then he rose up all of a sudden. "And don't buy anything else at Shabby's! No axes, no sleds, nothing!"

Sheriff Tom worked at his desk for the rest of the morning and then made his way down to the depot after lunch to find that the stage had come early and all of the passengers had already gone home. Standing there in the middle of the street, he scratched his head for a moment, thinking. He wanted to talk to Farmer Jackson, but it could wait until the morning if necessary. The most important thing was getting that boot, but that also required waiting until morning.

Just then, he looked down the road to see Trapper Jones walking straight toward him. Surprised, he stepped forward to meet him.

"Jones?" he said, peering up at the bearded man. "What brings you into Smithy?"

"I had to tell you something that may help in your investigation," Jones said, glancing around a bit uncomfortably as if he was unused to being out in the open. "Law dog," he added a bit spitefully when Tom began to smile.

"Well, it's you coming to me," the sheriff said easily. "Anyhow, I didn't bribe you, so I'm happy to see you turning over a new leaf."

"I ain't never had a guilty conscience, and I'm not about to start," Jones said in a stiff tone. Then he changed his voice to sound calmer and said, "You know Mr. Brown had a problem with a thief that broke in some months ago, and he hired me to track him down. There were two of them, one with a patched eye who took a shot at me, and a terrible shot he was. The other must have known about me, because he took off fast, and then they got in a tub and went down the river."

"The second must have known about you? What does that mean?" Sheriff Tom asked, more to himself, but definitely out loud.

"I own the trapping these parts, and I'm the best tracker and the best shooter in the whole county!" Jones said proudly. "He knew he didn't stand a chance, so when his partner started shooting, he took off."

"I see," Tom said, nodding. "Makes sense, but what happened after that?"

"Well, when Brown and I reached the bend where they threw in their tub, he told me it wasn't worth going any further. I could see them a far way off, and the way they were heading into the rapids before the waterfall told me they didn't know how to steer, and I wouldn't be surprised if they didn't know how to swim neither."

The sheriff just listened quietly to all of that and then nodded. "Well, Jones, I appreciate it. You supposing they drowned?"

"Likely," Jones said and then said nothing else.

"Well," Tom said after a moment. "No time to lose then, because I don't think one of them drowned and I know just where he is." He put out his hand. "Thank you, Jones, and have a good day."

Jones pulled his hand away sharply, staring after the sheriff with surprise. Then he followed, walking quickly to keep up. "You say one of them survived? Just one?"

"That's what I said," Tom said sharply and then whirled about. "Jackson's place. You coming to help find him?"

"Well—"

"No money!" barked the sheriff sharply, seeing why the trapper hesitated. "This is county business! Law and order! You're either on the good side or the bad side! Which will it be?"

"I'll help," Jones said stiffly without any more hesitation and followed the sheriff into the little office to get some more supplies.

The afternoon sun was beginning to go down when Sheriff Tom and Trapper Jones reached the woods beyond the Jackson farm. They easily found Jim's trail when they spotted an old brown coat sitting behind a bush and took off after his tracks.

After a few minutes, Trapper Jones began to suggest going further up the hill so they could see further along the riverbed, but the sheriff refused and doggedly kept on the path for about a mile until they came to a pile of leaves and sticks with an odd misshapen cross sticking out on top.

The sheriff stopped quickly and stood there for a moment, and then looked at Jones. "Seen this before?"

"Not in my life," Jones said, a bit puzzled. "Someone set up church here?" He pointed to a small box against the base of a tree. "The poor box?"

Tom walked up to the box and opened it. Inside, he found several pieces of paper. "The Gold Maps of Adamsville," he read, a bit puzzled. "I heard about this legend but never knew if it existed. And look here, a note, 'Found, Fall 1858'. I suppose if that gold did exist, it is found now and spread out all around the county."

Jones stood nearby, his boot on a fallen log, and said nothing as he looked around in all directions. Finally, he said, "Well, shall we go on?"

"One moment," Tom said solemnly, going over to the pile with the cross on top and beginning to remove some of the branches. After a couple of minutes of digging on his own, he uncovered something that was wrapped up in a blanket, hesitated, and then immediately began to cover it back up.

"I believe we have found Robert," Sheriff Tom said, standing up and brushing off his hands.

"Robert?" Jones said, confused. "Who's that?"

"Jim's partner," Tom said in the same serious voice. Turning, he picked up the box and tucked it under his arm. "Evidence," he said and then began walking further down the river.

"I will need Doc Benson to come and do a thorough investigation, but based on the smell and the shape, there is no mistaking. And based on the fact that we are still before the falls, I am beginning to have serious doubts about this young Jim."

"You mean," Jones said, beginning to understand, "that there has been murder in Adamsville?" Taking a better grip on his axe, he began to appear angry. "Well, I will not stand for this! I don't know about you law dogs, but there will be no murderer getting away with crime in Adamsville! We'll hunt him down and string him up!"

"And there will be no lynching in Buck's County!" Sheriff Tom barked in a very stern voice. "We will find him, but we will not take matters into our own hands! We will bring him to the proper authorities!"

Jones grumbled something under his breath and allowed the sheriff to take the lead, appearing as if he would fade away into the woods but simply following at a distance.

As the woods grew darker, the sheriff spotted a figure stumbling along through the woods in the distance. As they grew nearer, the person spotted them and began running, appearing terrified.

"It's him!" Jones said suddenly, quite near the sheriff's ear. "Shall I shoot?"

"No," Tom said, "he is too exhausted. We will get him easily."

Just then, the young man stumbled and fell headlong into the mud, exhausted and miserable.

"There is our man," Tom said, turning to Jones. "He knows you, so you better stay back. I'll get him myself. Thank you for your help, sir, and I shall expect you in Smithy tomorrow."

"I'll be there," Jones said sharply. "I wouldn't miss it for anything." With that, he turned to disappear behind a nearby tree and watched as the sheriff went on alone toward the young man who lay moaning in the mud.

Sheriff Tom walked up to Jim and knelt down. "All right, Jim, are you going to come peaceably, or do I need to use force?"

"P-p-peaceably, sir, sheriff, sir," Jim gasped, slowly getting up.

"Good lad," Tom said, taking him by the arm to help him up and then pointing the way that he was to walk.

As the woods became covered in darkness, the sheriff and the sad young man made their way slowly back to the village.

Early the next morning, Deputy Steve walked in and seated himself at the typewriter. He was dressed very finely in a clean shirt and clean jeans, and he had even polished up his boots, belt, and hat for the occasion. It was a somber event, but it had to be done.

Sheriff Tom stood by the desk, waiting as everyone filed into the little office and seated themselves in the chairs set up in a row. Farmer and Mrs. Jackson were there, Mr. Brown was there, Trapper Jones was there, and several curious bystanders including Murphy, the village barber, and a couple of gossipy old women. It was time for the witnesses to present their case, and then the details would be sent to the circuit judge who was currently in another county. The judge would determine the severity of the crime and then send word when he would be able to come to hear the case thoroughly and give a sentence to the prisoner.

"My good people of Smithy, Coatestown, Adamsville, and surrounding," Sheriff Tom began, "this is indeed a sad day, but let us be honest before God and before these witnesses and tell the truth as we know it about this prisoner, Peter James Ramsey, or Jim, as he is known in this area, and the sad situation surrounding his partner-in-crime, Robert O'Duff."

With that, the sheriff sat down and nodded to his deputy to take over.

"Mrs. Sally Jackson," Steve called and she came up to sit in one of the chairs against the wall so that she could be seen by everyone in the room. She looked at the sheriff for a moment and then shook her head sadly, beginning to talk as the typewriter steadily kept up with her words.

"Well, Jim is such a nice young man, he showed up when my husband went down to Garbey to fix his plow and helped around the farm. He didn't cause any trouble at all and I gave him a nice place to stay in the barn and gave him some food. Poor Jim was so polite and kind and went into Smithy with me to pick up supplies and I introduced him to Sheriff Tom. I was worried about him, maybe he was sick or something, but I had no idea that such a horrible thing was weighing on his thoughts. I am so sad to hear that he is a thief and a murderer—" She stopped at that, shook her head, and refused to go on.

"Thank you, ma'am," Steve said as his typing came to a stop, and then he called out, "Mr. Brown."

Mr. Brown came up to take Mrs. Jackson's place and sat down, fiddling with his hat in his hands. "The prisoner broke into my house a couple of months ago, earlier this spring," he began, and then coughed a bit before going on. "He wasn't a terrible fellow, even for a thief, but he was really quite timid and didn't disturb anything. We fought a little in the house and I took his boot and found a fork he had thrown out the window. I suppose he fell into a lot of bad times to be so hard off."

"Stick to the facts, sir," Deputy Steve interjected.

"Yes, sir," Brown replied, nodding and thinking for a moment. "Well, he was going to take some of my private possessions, but he only got away with an old piece of paper that I was keeping as a souvenir. I came to the sheriff's for help, and I brought the boot and the fork, but they were too busy."

He stopped again, appearing a bit embarrassed at what he was about to say. "Well, so I asked Trapper Jones to help me track him down. We found him and his partner in the woods, and the little one with the patch took a shot at us but missed cleanly, and then they got away in a tub. When I told Jones that they didn't take anything, we decided to let them go and went back home. I hadn't seen anything about him after then."

"Thank you," Deputy Steve said, finishing up that line and turning to a new paragraph. "Trapper Jones."

Jones came up to the chair before the desk a bit nervously, looking around and feeling out of sorts because his gun and axe were back by the door. He kept his hat on and sat down stiffly, staring around at the sheriff and the deputy sheriff before speaking.

"I say that murder is murder and the law must be carried out. I know that prisoner plainly as I know my own boots, and he is the one that Mr. Brown and I tracked through the woods after he tried to rob his house."

He hesitated for a moment and then said, "The sheriff and I found the body of his partner buried beside the riverbank before the falls, and I found their tub further downstream after the falls. One of my friends, Ole Bixby, and his son saw the tub floating down the stream with no one in it and I took it ashore, but nothing was in it except for an old frying pan. Mark my words but murder has happened and this prisoner clearly deserves to die. The law must be plainly carried out and no law dog is worth his salt if he won't enforce the law!"

Without another word, Jones rose and marched to the back of the room, picking up his gun and axe and standing by the door, waiting to see what would happen.

"Thank you," Steve said, a bit breathlessly as he finished typing. Then he turned and looked at Sheriff Tom, who nodded. Steve looked at the people assembled. "Now the prisoner, Peter James Ramsey, will come and testify."

Tom went into the back to bring out Jim. The prisoner was looking a bit better this morning, but had refused to eat anything that day and would not look at anyone except down at his mismatched boots. Tom sat him in the chair and then nodded to Steve.

Jim, as he was known, awkwardly leaned over, his tied hands dangling between his knees. He stared down at the floor and then raised his head slightly, beginning to talk in a sad tone of voice.

"I know I'm a bad thiever, and I'll admit to that plainly, but I ain't never killed no one, especially not my best friend Robert." He took a deep breath and went on. "Robert was the worst rapscallion I ever knew, but I had to take care of him because of his poor eye that got knocked out in an accident, and I did take care of him, even though he was a hard fellow to get along with sometimes."

Jim paused and then said sadly, "I wish he was back instead of being killed. I know he was a little dumb, but he was a good fellow and a fine friend and always had my back." Then he shrugged and looked at Sheriff Tom to see if he could leave as the people began to talk in low whispers.

"Killed?" asked Tom, standing slowly and raising his hand to quiet the people. "What do you mean that Robert was killed?"

Jim struggled for a moment to control himself, but then he said angrily, "He was shot in cold blood murder for revenge!" Silence came over the group as the people faced the combined shock of his sudden change of tone and his information about Robert's unfortunate death.

Taking the opportunity, Jim stood up and faced the people, about to explain himself further. Then he gasped, seeing Jones standing by the door with his gun, axe, and black hat shoved on his head.

"Trapper Jones!" Jim choked a bit in surprise and then cried out, "The murderer! There he is!"

All the people looked in surprise from Jim to Jones and both Sheriff Tom and Deputy Steve leaped to their feet. A dark look came over Trapper Jones' face and he immediately stormed out of the building, Sheriff Tom hot on his heels. Deputy Steve gave a great sigh and sat down at the desk, looking at his notes.

Jim also sat down slowly and then looked up at Farmer and Mrs. Jackson who came to stand in front of him.

"Deputy, sir," said Jackson quietly, "while the deliberations with Trapper Jones are going on, my wife and I would like to request that we bring this here Jim—er, Peter James Ramsey—the prisoner, you see, that we bring him to our farm and take good care of him until the judge has time to come by."

Deputy Steve looked at all of them carefully and then nodded. "All right, you can do that. We know how to find you," he added with a bit of a chuckle. Then he stood up and shook Jackson's hand. "Good honest fellow, thank you," he said with a smile. "I know you and Mrs. Jackson will do a fine job with that poor lad."

So, Farmer and Mrs. Jackson brought Jim to their place, and in no time at all, he was learning to work hard. After a couple of days of rest and recovery, he was building up some fine callouses and muscles. Every day, someone passing by could see him working in the garden, hoeing or digging or pitching and sweating away, and they could hear him muttering to himself.

"Oh, I wish I was back to the free and easy times of thieving with Robert and didn't have to do this confounded work." He would wipe the back of his hand on his sweaty forehead and stop, giving a sigh as he looked up and down the garden row. Then he would remember his lunch pail in the shade of the nearby apple tree and grin.

"But the Jacksons are mighty fine folks to take me on and feed me and let me do my own exploring now and again."

After thinking a bit more, he would throw down his tool and walk to the end of the row to sit down in the nice fresh grass in the shade and pull out his lunch.

"As my father always said," he concluded, uncovering the food in the little pail with a grin, "'A fine honest job is better than all the gold earned by all the thieving in the whole world', and it even gets you a free lunch." With that, Jim chomped into his sandwich and smiled as he chewed away.

4

The Nobleman's Conflict

The overshadowing clouds were just becoming tinged with pink when the warrior finally lowered his sword. He took several deep breaths, feeling the adrenaline subside from coursing through his veins and leaving his body weary.

It had been a dreadful night. The enemy had come upon the city unexpectedly just before nightfall and had been relentless in their thirst for blood. But now, their host lay scattered across the plain—dead, wounded, or fleeing in every direction.

Lord Dunavin's cramped fingers relaxed their grip on the blood-encrusted sword and he released yet another tired breath. Turning toward the east, his glazed eyes took in the welcome sight of the quickly approaching dawn.

Time finally seemed to return, and sweetly. At last, the young nobleman could allow himself to rest. He stood there in the hush, his ears ringing, not yet able to distinguish the sounds of the birds in the far-off trees, not yet willing to acknowledge the groans of the wounded. He swept a weary hand over his brow and dropped his sword point to touch the ground in front of him. He had earned his rest.

As the sky continued to lighten before him, the noises behind him gently increased, replacing the miserable sounds of woe with the jingle of reigns and the creaking of carts as men and women from the fortress came to the rescue of the wounded.

A feeling of annoyance brushed over him and Dunavin lifted his trusty sword again, striding away across the field toward the east. He finally stopped on the edge of the carnage and found a quiet rock jutted out from the terrain, sinking down upon it. How long he sat there, Lord Dunavin did not know, nor did he care. He wished to remain alone, now, and give himself time—time to think, time to grieve, time to rest.

His time was too quickly interrupted by the sound of a person approaching. Turning his head away from the sound, he contemplated rising again and fleeing yet further but found himself unable to summon the strength to move.

"Water, my lord?"

His thoughts were immediately arrested and all sensations of bitterness fled from his mind. Eagerly, Dunavin turned in the direction of the youthful voice. Water. How long had it been that he had something to drink besides the sweat that ran in rivulets down his face and the blood of the enemy that splattered upon everything without regard?

A young peasant lad stood before him, his sleeves rolled up, lifting a dipper up from a bucket of water held in front of his tattered trousers.

"Yes," he said, suddenly breathless, taking the dipper from the boy's hand and gulping desperately—once, twice—it took four draughts before he was satisfied. Handing back the dipper to the lad, he caught his eyes on his face and noted how timidly he cast his glance to the ground. Inclining his head gratefully, Dunavin turned to face the morning light once more. The young man moved on, his footfalls quiet but determined in his quest to assist the needy.

Breathing in deeply, the lord closed his eyes as the first streaks of orange and gold flashed across the sky. Soon, very soon, the sun would rise and cast its face across the gory fields. It would be a day of hard work ahead for the common folk, who would be required to bury the dead carcasses of the enemy soldiers, to bring in the brave men who died for the safety of the fortress, to identify the bodies before giving them a proper burning, to care for the wounded.

Once again, a feeling of contentment that his work was over washed over the young lord. Once again, his mind turned to other weightier matters, deeper issues, subjects regarding life and death, law and order, peace and justice.

The rapid beats of a horse's hooves sounded behind him, and then someone slid down from the beast and called in a raspy voice, "Sire!"

He turned at that, immediately recognizing the voice of one of his most faithful men. Staggering to his feet, he grasped for his sword, but it was lying on the ground. Ignoring that, he lifted his head to face his comrade-in-arms.

Meeting the man's frank gaze and holding it for a moment, Dunavin understood the message without the need for words to pass between them. The scattered reports brought in battle had been true. Their leader had finally died in the early dawn. For him, it was over. In this life, their leader was gone—forever.

Nodding, Dunavin turned away. He looked down at the ground, took in a deep breath, and looked up at the sky which was brilliant in colors. Waving his hand aside impatiently as his servant stepped up beside him, he answered in a harsh-sounding voice that did not sound like his own.

"I'll come—later. Get some rest. We—I'll summon the council tonight—we'll talk then."

"Yes, my lord," the man said quietly and then turned aside, stepping over a carcass to swing himself back into the saddle and take off for the castle once more.

Stepping forward heavily, the grieved nobleman bent to pick up his sword. He studied it for a moment, thinking of all the times he had lifted it to follow their leader fearlessly in battle. A feeling of hopelessness and frustration came upon him and he cast his sword down again. Dropping down wearily upon the rock, his head came to rest between his soiled hands and Dunavin let out yet another deep sigh.

The news would travel fast. Shouts of victory would be turned into wails of grief. Hope would be traded for fear. The collection of images that flashed through his mind felt suddenly very distant and unreal, and yet, he knew the numbness to be a familiar sensation associated with the strange company named Death.

"My lord."

He opened his eyes and blinked as if waking out of a deep sleep. A peasant woman was standing before him, stooping slightly to look into his face, to check on him.

Struggling upward, he passed a hand over his head and sought to rid himself of the weariness. How he came to be lying on the ground with his head on the rock, he had not a clue.

"What is it?" he asked, his voice gruff and thick, sitting up and looking squarely at the female in front of him.

"Something to eat, my lord," she said quietly. She was another simple peasant and the hours of work among the wounded and survivors had rendered her clothing hopelessly soiled with dirt and blood. Her face was smudged as well, and wisps of hair had escaped from their binds.

He blinked and swallowed, watching as she lifted the lid of a rough pot over her arm, dipping a wooden bowl into its depths and handing it to him. The aroma of stew hit his nostrils and he was suddenly ravenous, jerking the bread from her hand that she offered from a bag over her shoulder. He ate hungrily, having forgotten about food for some time but the first taste bringing back all the memories he needed to respond.

When he looked up again, she was facing away and studying the sky. The sun seemed to be casually floating amidst the clouds, serenely casting its warm glow over the sodden and miserable wreckage caused by the night before.

"More, Sire?" she wondered, feeling his gaze upon her and turning back, her manners polite but aloof.

He held out the bowl and nodded, but his attitude had been placated by the food. "Our leader—you heard?" he asked, dipping more bread into the fresh stew, half-wondering why he deigned himself to discuss such matters with a peasant woman.

"Yes, Sire," she said humbly and then turned to study the sky again. She seemed to sigh, then, and said in a tone of awe, "At last, his soul has escaped and is free—free at last—free to soar with the birds—praise be to the Lord."

The man lowered the bowl and looked at the peasant with a mixture of surprise and bewilderment as he chewed and swallowed.

"And where," he demanded, "did you come up with that fine sentiment, girl?"

She turned a pair of nervous eyes toward him and then looked down upon the ground once more without answering. He stared at her as he ate, noting her strong forearms, the easy way with which she carried the heavy pot, and her simple clothing. She was nothing more than a peasant, brought up in the rough and squalid homes of the poor class, and yet, even the peasants knew of the changes that this battle had ushered in.

"Who are you?" he wondered, shifting his weight on the hard ground to lean against the rocks and handing the bowl back to her. "What are you?"

The woman looked down at him, her expression still uneasy and timid. "I am the daughter of a farmer, my lord, and the wife of a farmer, as well," she said simply and turned away.

"Stay," Dunavin commanded, not knowing yet what he would say next. His hesitation did not last long. "You are but a farmhand, and yet you have deep thoughts. How can this be?"

"Even the meanest of folk are free to think, my lord," she replied demurely, her eyes still upon the ground.

"All are free to think, yes, but to think well, that is certainly a different matter." He grasped for his sword and leaned upon it as he rose unsteadily. Stepping up to stand beside the girl, he glanced down at her curiously, the top of her head not even reaching his shoulder. Looking down the length of his sword, he inspected it for a moment and then slid it into its sheath at his side.

"Now, tell me, O peasant woman, you who are free to think, what do you foresee? Now that our leader is dead, what shall happen to our city and its fields and forests, what shall happen to our common folk and noblemen alike?"

Her young face was lifted quickly, a look of dismay crossing her features. "I am no prophet, my lord. I cannot foretell the future!"

"Nay, not foretell the future, girl," he said impatiently, putting out his hand lest she attempt to flee. "But a peasant who speaks of such matters as a soul leaving its wretched body—surely you have an opinion on the matter." The man looked down at her pointedly.

"Oh, Sire, I meant no disrespect toward our leader—may he rest in peace," she said uneasily, stepping away from him.

"But he was wretched!" the warrior said passionately, his teeth gritted together in a restrained rage. "Everyone saw it. Everyone knew it. I saw it! I knew it! And what could I do? I could do nothing!"

Calming himself with an effort, he looked at the young woman steadily for a moment and then asked in a subdued tone, "Are you frightened?"

"Yes, Sire," she admitted, her hands trembling as they desperately clung to the handle of the stew pot. She backed away further. "My lord, I must see to the others." She lifted her face, her eyes pleading.

"Go, then," he said, waving her away. Frustrated, he wished to sit down again and return to his sleep where matters of political unrest would not assail him, but he caught sight of a pair of horses approaching swiftly. Recognizing one of the steeds as the warhorse of his brother-in-arms, Leopold, he waited.

"Lord Dunavin!" The man's sharp eyes were relieved. "We have been searching for you everywhere! We feared that—but never mind that now, your presence is required at the castle. The Mistress—the Lady in Black seeks you now."

Dunavin's face was suddenly impatient. "She does, does she?" he muttered under his breath. Catching the reins of the other horse, he swung himself into the saddle with an effort. Meeting the eyes of his comrade, he caught the light of understanding there. He leaned over and grasped Leopold's arm in greeting and brotherly affection.

"Ride with me now, brother," Dunavin said shortly, tugging at the reins. "We will face this calamity together."

"I am afraid I cannot, Sire, though it would rejoice my heart greatly to do so. I am in search of the others."

Dunavin nodded. "Go then, and meet me in the King's Room tonight. Indeed, tonight, we shall hold council."

Leopold gave him a short nod and raised his hand in salute before quickly cantering away.

A huddle of servants met Lord Dunavin at the gate and whisked him away into a private room for a bath and a clean change of clothes. As he reclined in the bath, the warm water relaxing his tired muscles, he contemplated lingering there for the remainder of the day. However, his thoughts did not permit him to rest for any length of time, particularly when he remembered the council that would be formed that evening.

Dragging himself upward from the warmth of the bath, he felt the cool sting of the air and snatched up a towel hastily. Calling for his clothes, he dressed himself impatiently and then, seeing that a page had not finished cleaning his boots, snatched up a pair of cloth shoes instead.

"My lord," an elderly servant appeared at the door. "The mistress requires—"

"I have no time," he snarled, swiping the towel off his head and shaking the damp curls from his eyes. He hurled the towel to the floor and turned toward the back doorway, intent on escaping the ever-present demands of the ominous Lady in Black. Dunavin made his way up the stairway by two and three steps at a time. It was a strange irony, for not only was there one woman after him, but he had another woman to find.

After a half-hour's search and careful avoidance of guards and servants, Dunavin found her on the rampart overlooking the city.

He made his way toward her swiftly, his footfalls echoing across the quiet castle roof.

She was dressed in a light green robe, her hands resting lightly on the wall in front of her, her cloak and veil discarded at her side, leaving her hair free and floating lightly in the breeze. The morning sun embraced her in all its brilliance and left her appearing full of youth and vigor.

Turning her head slightly so her profile was visible to him, she said serenely, "My lord, I am contented to see you well and whole after such a battle."

"How can you tell that I am indeed well and whole?" Dunavin demanded with a sudden savagery that surprised him. "You are not even looking upon me now!"

Still calm, she inclined her head gravely. "I have been here since dawn, Sire."

"Mocking the day, I suppose." He came to stand beside her and looked at the tall, slim woman narrowly. "And what mysteries have you discovered here, Madam, while the sun mounts higher and higher into the sky and the woe and doom that enshrouds the city grows darker and darker?"

At that, the Lady Penelope turned her fair face in his direction, her clear eyes piercing his. "My lord, I implore you, be not so bitter!" Her mournful look lasted but a second, for she faced the sun again and lifted both arms toward the sky with a radiant smile.

"The battle is won, my lord, and though it were a bitter night for all, the morning has brought joy! For behold, the soul that long lay imprisoned has been released! He has been released from utter torment and is now free! He is free from the misery and woe of earthly pains and sorrows and shall now go forth with rejoicing!"

"You speak of our leader, I see," he said solemnly, his tone not at all matching hers. He stared at the Lady Penelope in silence for a moment and was suddenly reminded of the peasant woman who had spoken in a similar vein of joy and relief. The same questions as before rushed through his mind and Dunavin hoped that he would at last receive some answers to his queries.

"But where, I ask you, where do the souls go? Where is he now?"

The maiden turned to Lord Dunavin and said with an unconcerned shrug, "I know not, my lord, for it is no concern of mine, nor yours. The Lord God of heaven and earth, it is He who has created the soul and breathes life into the body, uniting them as one, and it is He who calls back the soul to leave the body lifeless for a time. He knows, and that is enough."

"Enough for you, perhaps." His words came out as a growl and he paced away from her for several yards in disappointment. Then he returned, seating himself indecorously on one of the stone pillars that scattered the rooftop, glaring up at her. "But what of all the others? Yes, what of his wife, the Lady in Black, as she is now called? What say you of her?"

A slight shadow crossed the fair face and she gazed far across the fields stretching toward the east. "I see no hope there, Sire. Only the Lord knows that answer, and only He can bring grace and repentance to her embittered soul."

Turning to him swiftly, Penelope said imploringly, "But think not of such dark things, Sire! Rest you now, I pray, and upon the morrow there shall be time and opportunity to consider what shall be accomplished. The city shall recover, and then," here her face became radiant again, "then *you* shall be our leader, my good lord!" At those words, she inclined her head toward him reverently.

"Me? Bah!" He leaped to his feet and made as if to dash all her words away. "You know well that I am not fit to be such a leader! I am too bold, too brash, too impetuous, too reckless, too wild! You know these things that people say, and quite well, I would add."

In a lower tone, he concluded, "And particularly because I have devised means for the ultimate rebellion in her eyes—that is, I would restore those things which were removed in times past. I would seek out the old alliances that were previously deemed hasty and unwise."

Her face flushed with excitement as the realization of his secret words fell upon her ears. "Oh, but my lord!" Passion rose in her voice as she turned back to him, and she spoke on, boldly, though her hands trembled. "You cannot, you must not hold on tightly to what others say! You know—in your heart of hearts, you know!— that you are right and that the others are wrong! And, Sire, furthermore, you know that they have no more power, now that our leader has passed, they cannot remain in power now. For thus says the law, that it is now yours to command, O lord."

"They have no more power, you say," Lord Dunavin spoke softly, his eyes a gleam of restrained fire. "No more power." Turning aside, he smiled a bit, though without humor. "We shall see what power they still wield, be it theirs to command or mine. You well know the tyranny of late, and whether that power be true or devised, it is still there. It will not be an easy battle to win."

Pacing about, the man suddenly stopped in a terror of realization. "What madness do I speak!" he said violently, "I want no power!" Turning swiftly back to the silent woman, he went on savagely, "You have seen what power does to a man, to a woman, to a group of men who are given time and opportunity!

"You have seen what it does to a man in his lust to become something which he is not, how it cripples him, bows him down as a withered tree, and how it eventually kills him!

"You still see what it does—to her! How she expands herself daily with judgments and reckonings, how there is none that does right in her sight, how she alone is perfection, and even the power that she has is not enough!

"And the lackeys that surround her," here he swore angrily, "you say they have no power! Never have they had the full power they desire and never have they had the limited power they deserve! What do they deserve, you ask? To be thrown down from the highest cliff until they tremble in true repentance and compassion for fellow man!"

All at once, he ceased speaking, his heated face immediately cooling. "My lady," he said soberly, inclining his head toward her, "I must depart. I have summoned the council to gather tonight, and I must prepare."

He turned abruptly on his heel and made for the stairs, but suddenly paused and turned back. "My lady—"

Penelope silently moved to face him, her expression bright and steady. "Yes, my lord."

"Remain in prayer, my faithful sister," he said in a low and uncharacteristically emotional tone and then whirled about, his broad shoulders disappearing around the corner of the stone wall.

Drawing in a deep breath, the lady turned back toward the sun. "Indeed, I shall, my lord, and in time you shall be adequately prepared for speech, and for action." She smiled a bit and then lowered her voice to speak into the breeze, "For full well you know that he who wants power least deserves it most. Yes, she wants power, she has always wanted it.

"But it is *yours*, O Dunavin, and *you* shall succeed. Perhaps you shall restore the old alliances now, but perhaps not for many years. That does not matter. What matters is that you tried your very best, and that you loved your people most, with humility, without arrogance, without the slightest regard for the idol of power. And, indeed, with the help of the Lord Almighty, you *shall* prevail."

Satisfied, she closed her eyes and lifted her hands toward the sunlight as if to embrace all the glory of the morning.

5
An Olden Tale of Heroism

In former days they told of tales of heroism and valor, and scurvy folk claim that those merry years were past long ago, yet not all is lost in these moons, for lived there once in a sliver of land by the bonny sea, a Knight surrounded by his kinfolk in a sprawling hut once constructed by an old fellow by the name of Master Dunn. Wild it was and fierce the sun on that jolly island, but lived they there for six fortnights in contentment and merriment until a great despondency came and swept a number of the souls into sadness and woe.

The littlest of them all were sent into a sprawling puzzlement and the wisest lords and ladies pondered on the best course of duty that would rescue their sprawling abode from the misery and gloom. Sat they one evening in the great hall where the sound of tears and whisperings could be heard all the way down the lane to the ears of the rogues who wished ill upon them all, commoner and nobleman alike.

As the clock began to strike the hour of midnight and not a resolution was to be found, the hearts of all save one had sunk into an abyss of darkness. For that one was the Knight of the House, a fine lad of short stature but of a great heart and no despondency could cause him to quiver or shake in his boots. Looked he around upon the distress of his kinfolk and his ears did catch the noise of the scurvy rogues chortling out in the lane, and a fierce wroth entered his great heart and a black cloud crossed his countenance.

Now see! Leaped he up that true Knight with a sudden bound to snatch up his sword and release a great and determined cry:

"A Sebastian!"

And sprang he out into the darkness of the night, disappearing into the gloom where his kinfolk were afraid to venture but slightly.

Yet a hush fell upon the darkened island and what was not known remained unknown for a great time of anguish and uncertainty, until, at last, the dawn's faint glow revealed a hero upon the horizon.

Behold! It was the faithful Sir Sebastian! Now carried he his stained sword and wore he his tattered coat and boots with a cloak of weariness, but reentered he the great hall with a soaring spirit of victory and peace. The devil and his league had verily been vanquished from the seashore and his bonny kinfolk were safe from harm thusly.

Astonished were they all at his appearance and even more so from his triumphant victory, that the hush remained as the hero retook his seat upon the dusty hearth and began to clean and polish his true sword.

Lo! A soft rap at the portal, and the Knight turned to see a fair and merry Lady crossing the threshold with a goodly bowl of mead, for she had heard of the dark night and traveled all dawn upon the wings of the morn to reach his side. Glad was his heart and gladder his voice and raised he up his oracle with a bonny tune.

By and by, the whole host of his kinfolk began to rejoice with him and celebrate the victory with full glasses of a goodly ale brought up from the well-stocked larder for such a jolly occasion that warranted true festivity.

Deed and indeed, the merrymaking continued forthwith until the goodly sun rose to his full stature that day, casting he his kindly rays upon the jolly sight of the merry Nobleman and his happy kith and kin. For peace had come to the sprawling house upon the seashore and wouldst remain for a time, times, and half a time until finally coming to the place verily known as

The End.

6

Lord Leo and the Violoncello

Once upon a time, long and far away, in the land of the Jamboree, lived a magnificent musician named Lord Leopold the Mad Cellist. He owned a great number of splendid instruments that he would order his minions to carefully tune and polish for three hours, five days a week. Then on the sixth day, he would choose his favorite cello, carefully pack it up in a specially padded black bag, put it in a fine coach that was driven by the fastest steeds and the most attentive footmen, and ride it all the way to another kingdom where people would come from far and wide to hear his splendid music.

Well, life went on for some time like this, with much enjoyment from everyone, and every year, money came pouring in so that Lord Leo, as his adoring fans lovingly called him, could purchase better instruments and finer music to practice. Also, songwriters from far and wide would come and beg Lord Leo to practice their music to see if it would stand the test of time. Sadly, not many songwriters were that good, but occasionally, Lord Leo would find someone that he greatly appreciated and hire them to come and help him improve his style. Such is the world of famous music, apparently.

Then, one unsuspecting day, tragedy struck, as most stories tell, because otherwise, stories would not be very interesting.

Lord Leo woke on the second day of the week, dressed in a splendid fashion, ate a leisurely breakfast, and then took a stroll out to his Piano Piazza where he was accustomed to climbing 88 steps to practice on his grand piano for one hour and forty-five minutes exactly. Then, when the bell struck, he rose solemnly, walked to the top of the stairs, and then turned giddy with joy as he cracked his knuckles with glee and galloped down the winding staircase as fast as his little legs could carry him.

Well, here was the best part of his day. Time to practice the violoncello! Lord Leo loved his Cello Castle best of all. It had four floors, and he would play a different kind of music on each floor. His favorite floor was the very top one since it overlooked all of his beautiful lands and he felt very noble and dignified, playing for his entire property. All the people would stop working, wherever they were in the fields, gardens, and buildings, and listen and smile, for they were happy to hear the music of Lord Leo.

But today, there was a problem. A servant met Lord Leo at the door of the Cello Castle, wringing her hands, tears streaming down her face. Lord Leo stopped and looked puzzled, and he felt awkward because he did not know what to do when servants cried.

"What is wrong, my good fiddle?" Lord Leo wondered, since he called all his servants silly names like that. The woman began to say something, but then she covered her face with her hands and ran away, past Lord Leo, down the path as fast as she could go.

Lord Leo was very confused, but then he noticed that the castle was very quiet. He did not hear the usual sound of polishing and tuning. Everything was deathly quiet. His face began to turn white as he nervously entered the first hall of the first floor. And then he gasped.

His favorite cello was gone!

He looked around, but all of his servants had vanished. He went up to the spot where he always put it, and there was the stand, but where was the cello?

Now he understood why his servants had run away. He sat down at the nearest seat and began to feel very depressed as he thought about what to do. As he thought and thought, a little tinge of red began to appear on his ears and spread across his whole face until he was as red as a fat beet.

Then Lord Leo knew what to do. He rose solemnly from his seat and went back to the door, reaching for the rope to a small bell that would summon his guard. He reserved the bell for very special occasions or in cases of emergency. He yanked the rope three times, and the bell clanged: Ding, Dang, Dong!

Soon, the sound of hooves clattered on the cobblestone, and Lord Leo stood in the doorway as a guard in clanking armor got off his horse, walked up, and saluted.

"Go summon my brother," Lord Leo said in a solemn voice. "Tell him my best violoncello is missing."

"Yes, sir!" said the soldier, and was about to leap back on his horse, when he stopped and looked confused. "Which brother, sir?"

"Earl Ernest of the Yankee Dune."

"Oh, yes, of course, sir!" said the soldier, and rode away as fast as the horse could carry him.

The soldier, whose name was Sir Stephen, felt a little stupid, because Earl Ernest was Lord Leo's closest brother, even though they sometimes fought, so he should have known which brother to summon. But he soon forgot about his mistake and rode on, over the hills and prairies until he saw a great sprawling house in the middle of a green field. He also heard a great commotion and smiled, knowing that the Earl would know who he was before he arrived.

Earl Ernest loved to hear news and tell news, so he had special spies posted all throughout the land, who would secretly report to one another until the news quickly traveled to a very important man that Earl Ernest hired three years ago and loved very much to keep next to him at all times so he could hear all the news of the day. That man's name was Frederick the Field Announcer.

So, when Sir Stephen arrived on the scene, Earl Ernest and his whole family were already gathered in front of the house, ready to hear what he had to say. Sir Stephen solemnly dismounted, but he was having a hard time not laughing, because Earl Ernest's house was always full of fun and merriment, and all of his children had a bad habit of running around with messy faces like happy, grubby urchins.

But before Sir Stephen could stop himself from smiling, Earl Ernest boomed forth in a jolly voice, "What news! What news! How is Lord Leo? How is his piano? How are his cellos?"

"Sad day, Sir Earl," Stephen said, forcing his face into a frown even though he still wanted to laugh.

"It is a sad day for Sir Earl!" Frederick suddenly announced, and Earl Ernest looked at him in shock and horror. Then he laughed and punched Frederick so hard that he went flying out of view. He often did that when Frederick got his facts wrong, and then he would have no field announcer for three hours, and by that time, Earl Ernest would forget all about the mistake and go looking for the man in the fishing pond so he could have some more news.

But anyway, Sir Stephen went on. "Lord Leo's favorite cello is missing. He has summoned you to help him."

Earl Ernest began to dance with glee. How dearly he loved to solve mysteries! He turned to his wife and children and all the servants standing around and they began to talk very loudly about what they would do.

Sir Stephen began tapping his foot. He had to get back to Lord Leo on the double, for he knew that Lord Leo would be pacing back and forth, fuming mad, and sending the rest of his soldiers all throughout the land with their swords and spears to steal everyone's instruments and hold them hostage until he got back his favorite cello. But no sooner had he tapped his foot three times, then Earl Ernest's servants were running everywhere, and all his family were scrambling for the carriage, and Earl Ernest was climbing onto his favorite steed, a fine, tall black horse with a pale spot on the end of his nose.

Earl Ernest was still shouting instructions as they rode away, and Sir Stephen sighed. Even though Lord Leo trusted his brother, sometimes he wondered if it would be better to summon someone else next time since it always turned into a loud party whenever Earl Ernest showed up on the scene, and that was not very helpful for practicing music.

But on and on they rode, and soon they reached Lord Leo, who had just begun to pace back and forth with steam coming out of his ears. Earl Ernest leaped down and began to talk very excitedly, asking many questions, but Lord Leo did not want to answer any questions, especially since he did not have the answers, so he glared at his brother and the two of them began to engage in a good old fashioned game of fisticuffs.

Meanwhile, Sir Stephen stood there and shook his head, but he was not surprised. Then he looked around and saw horses and carriages coming from everywhere, and then he was a little bit surprised since they seemed more numerous than Earl Ernest's family.

Presently, the great host gathered around Lord Leo and Earl Ernest, who were still fighting and hurling insults left and right, until one great lady who had a flowered hat got down from a carriage driven by a king with a greybeard and yelled, "Boys!"

Both of them immediately stopped and looked up and said at the same time in a surprised voice, "Mother!"

And then Lord Leo looked around in even greater surprise to see his whole family there! Even his father and mother, the King and Queen from the faraway land of Milk and Honey, had come! Lord Leo was very puzzled since he knew that it usually took everyone two weeks to travel to his lands, and he had not summoned them to help him with his mystery. But then, as he looked around at all his siblings, he saw that his beloved family had been plotting against him, and his ears turned red.

Before Lord Leo could think of anything to say, Earl Ernest was chattering in one ear and dancing with delight, and his younger sister Lady Lilly jumped out of her carriage and began chattering in his other ear, and soon he figured out the whole plan that they had been conspiring for weeks about how to surprise him!

But there was only one problem. "What about my favorite violoncello?" Lord Leo asked solemnly when all the chattering finally slowed down.

At that, he heard a snicker, and Lord Leo turned to see his three older brothers carrying a great case, and then Duke Dudley of the Dreadful Doons snidely said that he had stolen it in the night.

Lord Leo turned to Sir Stephen in surprise. "What!"

Sir Stephen simply stroked his beard and smiled a tiny bit. "I am sorry, sir, but the Queen sent a secret message and I could not dare to disobey her order."

Then another sister, Duchess Diana of the Flowered Field, came forward and handed him a card, saying in a very practical way, "We decided you would like this better since your other one really wasn't as good as you thought it was."

Lord Leo was even more surprised, and he was not sure if he was supposed to be insulted or glad, but he opened the card, and in it was a very careful explanation of the finest violoncello that his land of Jamboree had heard of. The instrument was apparently called Nelson's Sharpest, which he personally thought was a very odd name, but before he could think about that detail, there was the very cello in front of him, for his brothers had all taken it out of the case and placed it on a shiny new stand before his eyes.

Lord Leo was dumbstruck for the space of 45 seconds, and his eyes kept blinking and his mouth opening and closing, but then he leaped forward, snatched up his favorite bow, and began playing at a very great speed. It was such a beautiful sound that he wanted to sing and cry at the same time.

So, after playing one very fast song, he rose and bowed very deeply to his whole family, for he was gratified by their generosity and love for him, even if they caused him a great deal of stress from time to time.

His whole family clapped, and then his servants began reappearing with bright smiles on their faces and pulled out tables and chairs and great loaves of bread and hunks of meat and cakes and pies and squashes and fruits and cheeses and fine ales, and other foods of all sorts. So they sat down in the Great Halle and feasted for a time, and then Lord Leo solemnly rose and took his brand new violoncello up to the top of his four-floored castle, sat down carefully upon his little stool, and began to play one song after the next until the stars came out and all the tired people in the world lay down upon the sweet grass by the little campfires and went to sleep.

7

The Young Fellow and the Hermit

Once upon a time, in a faraway place in the deep woods, there was a shack in which an old hermit lived with all his books. He had a rather boring life, but the highlight was when a roaming young man would come and visit him once a week.

The young fellow always came by with a great sack of fine foods that he would cook up a fine feast with, and he would sit for hours and talk to the old man about all sorts of poetry and literature and fancy things that caused them to think and talk deeply.

It was a very grand time every week, for the young man was famous for bringing along fine foods and deep thoughts, and he was well-liked by all. But the most distinguished feature about this fellow was his cape that was made out of a genuine bearskin, beaten very thin, and his footwear that allowed him to run like lightning and walk in complete silence. And the sandals were true and faithful, but one day, they failed him.

It was a typical afternoon in the hermit's cabin and the hermit and his friend were dozing in their chairs by the hearth when there came an odd sound outside. Starting up, the young fellow poked the hermit politely, who simply grunted, made an unusual reference to Poe, and claimed that a bear was sniffing around outside because of the glorious meal they had just consumed.

"Shall I do anything about it?" the fellow wondered.

"Nah," Mr. Hermit said, stumbling up on his feet and reaching for the rifle above the door. "I'll teach him, and you shall make me my own cape!"

The young fellow considered that, and was about to respond when suddenly, the hermit dropped the rifle with a clatter.

"It's the BWC gang!" he said in horror, staring out the window.

"The what?"

"The BWC gang! Those kids come by every day and try to preach to me!"

"Preach?" The young fellow began to feel excited. "About what?"

"How do I know? But look! They have a Bible, that's why I called them the BWC gang, the Bible-Wielding Crazies gang!"

"What's wrong with Bibles?" the young fellow wondered, pointing to the books. "You have many!" And, he added to himself in disappointment, "And I thought he was coming closer to the Lord!"

The hermit grumbled, picking up the rifle again, and headed for the door. He jerked the door open and started to shout out angrily.

The young fellow was horrified and leaped to his feet, but all he saw was the BWC kids running away with fear.

"No! Wait!" he sprang for the door, determined to meet them.

And that was when his sandals failed him. When he sprang forward, he tripped, for one of his straps had become stuck in the floorboards.

The next thing the young fellow knew, he was rolling down hill, wrapped up in his cape with his sandal straps neatly trussing him up, and it was a fine fix!

But all's well that ends well, so they say. Even truly, it was divine providence that caused the young fellow to trip, fall, and roll down the hill.

For, when he hurtled down the hill, he caught up with the fleeing gang and they caught him in their arms with glee! In fact, they thought he was the nasty old hermit, so they carried him off and preached to him for a good half-mile.

Imagine their astonishment when they finally untrussed him, stood him up on his feet, and behold! It was not the old man! But the young fellow was so overjoyed that he asked to join their gang, and they were happy to have him.

By and by, the young fellow was able to introduce everyone to the old hermit, who, after much prayer and discussion, was finally converted. And best of all, in the end, they all had a great, fine, jolly feast, and were merry into the night.

8
Night Journey to Sanity's End

As told by Johnny McDuff

If you have never lost your sanity, consider yourself among the fortunate few who remain within the narrow margins of mental wholeness. As for me and my own life, I have since resigned myself to the fact that I shall never be normal again. Never, ever again shall I be able to enjoy the things that I once cherished. Forever and ever, I shall be forced to remember that horrible night when everything in my life and in my mind collapsed.

It was the fifth of July, during that mad summer that I found myself on the Jersey shores for a whole two weeks. Or was it the sixth? I cannot rightly recall, for it may have been either, as it was nighttime and certainly past midnight by the time the horrors came upon me. If you ever have lived in or visited Wildwood, New

Jersey, you would know what I mean when I say that time seems a foreign concept in that land.

In any event, there I was, that mad night, finding myself standing by the DQ at the end of the boardwalk and waiting. Waiting for what? I did not know rightly, myself, though I do believe I was wondering what had happened to my friend, Stuart, who had agreed to meet me there with a few others.

The tram cars were squealing up to their station, those wretched trundling machines of misery, and I stood there aimlessly as I watched the employees dismount and disappear into the ticket booth. I glanced down at my phone as an Asian girl came up to the ice-cream counter to order, brushing by me and having that zoned-out look that exhausted humans often wear.

I watched her sideways as I stood there, one hand jammed in my pocket, the other gripping my phone. She was drooping everywhere—from her shoulders, and her hands that reached out to take the shake that she had purchased, even to her jet-black ponytail that swung lazily sideways as she brushed by me again and disappeared into the crowd of pedestrians chattering all around us.

Once again, I glanced at my unanswered text and I remember sighing, though I cannot recall the hour or the minute that was displayed on the screen. Distinctly, however, I do know there was a rising frustration at having been forgotten by Stuart and our pals. Whether that frustration was right or wrong, I cannot tell, but it led me to give up.

Meandering down the line, I stood on the cement pavement and stared across the railing at the Wildwood Crest arch, watching as people streamed off the boardwalk and away to their motels and hotels and housing for the night. I heard the chattering in a variety of languages and once more felt displaced by time and space.

"Watch it, pal," a measured voice cut into my thoughts, and I turned to see a uniformed policeman standing between me and a slowly approaching tram car.

Blinking, I stepped away and muttered an awkward and embarrassed phrase of acknowledgment and gratitude. To my surprise, he came and stood beside me, his arms folded across his chest, staring as the last car squealed itself around the bend and came to a rest behind the line of trams waiting. Waiting for what?

"Where do they go at night?" I wondered, foolishly voicing my question aloud.

"What?" the cop responded, swiping a hand over his buzzed scalp. He set his cap back on properly and looked at me sideways. "Who?"

"The tram cars," I replied, motioning to the long line of idling machines. "Where do they go at night?"

"Oh, I don't know," he said dismissively. "Somewhere in the piers." His companion drove up at that moment in the police cart and he waved a casual farewell to me as he hopped up and they drove off.

Disappointed, I wandered along the railing and then paused to lean over and watch a drunken fool reel along below me in the sand, holding onto the boardwalk pillars for support. He stumbled aimlessly back and forth, mumbling to himself.

Laughing slightly, I felt a sudden kinship with him, a wave of unexpected grogginess making me want to stumble about wearily as well. "Where do the tram cars go at night?" I called over the railing to him, but he did not reply. Giving up on him as well, I stumbled away, feeling a peculiar daze come over me.

A moment or an hour could have passed in that segment of time that I simply stood there—and then I found myself stumbling forward again, my groping hands stretching out blindly until they touched cool metal. I felt a twinge of surprise, but then I was stepping up onto the nearest tram car and it registered in my feeble mind that I was about to discover the answer to my question, "Where do the tram cars go at night?"

Hunkering down in the car, I wished I could become invisible. I wanted neither to pay the fee nor to be seen riding the tram car by my corny friends. I merely wanted to satisfy my burning curiosity.

"Where do the tram cars go at night?" I mumbled once more to myself but then ducked down further rather violently as I saw a young man approaching jauntily. He must have gone into the driver's car for, presently, there was a small lurch, and then we were off. Fortunately for me, I was on the last car and it appeared that I had escaped undetected.

As we continued down the cement pathway, I cautiously raised myself and peered ahead, seeing the colors of the other trams some distance before mine—the red and white of the Coca-Cola cars and the yellow and blue regular ones. I looked to the left, seeing all the shop-keepers beginning to close up. The boards were nearly empty. The night was beginning to feel magical.

Gaining courage, I sat up stiffly in the seat, staring straight in front at the back of the young driver's head, wondering if he would catch sight of me in the rearview mirror.

Oh! If he only had seen me then! If only he had stopped the tram! If only he had sent me reeling off into the dark by myself! If only the truth of the tram cars had remained an eternal mystery! Then, and only then, would I be spared the everlasting misery of my current existence!

But I digress. The tram was rapidly picking up speed, and with it, I felt a rush of reckless abandon come over me. A pair of teens on bikes rode past us out of the misty ocean air and I stood up on shaky legs, waving wildly to them. I suddenly did not care if the young driver had spotted me, and as the teens disappeared, I caught a glimpse of his face in the rearview mirror.

I sat down again, studying him. The kid had an ordinary face, but the longer I stared at him, the more peculiar he appeared. There was something about his eyes. Was it my imagination or were they really glowing? Were they red? Or orange? Or green? Or blue? Or were they an indeterminate color like the funky neon lights that shone up and down and all around the shops on the boards? Truly they could not have been white—hot white—like the burning sensation that was beginning somewhere below my sternum?

Shaking my head to clear it, I rose again, feeling a weariness crash over me without warning. I wondered what time it was, but did not bother to take my phone from my pocket, as it took all my strength and effort to remain upright. Distinctly, I remember feeling that I had been on that tram car all night long.

I relented in my fight against the exhaustion and seated myself again, slumping forward wearily and permitting my eyelids to drift closed. The gentle trundling of the car continued, rocking me off into a restless daze. Time seemed to become further and further a thing of mystery and uncertainty.

The car jolted slightly, and I sat up quickly, my eyelids popping open. Taking in a deep breath, I felt disappointed as everything appeared the same as before—the boards, the lights, the silence— save for the hum and screech of the machine underneath me and the rhythmic jolting as the wheels trundled over the uneven cement. Were we going faster than before? Or was it only my imagination taking over again? I looked left and right, seeing the shops going on and on for miles, it seemed, but everything was increasingly blurry and misty before my eyes.

A twinge of nausea crept over me, and I wished to go home and be in my bed. It was too late and too much to be traveling in this constant motion on the boards. Could I rise and depart from the wretched tram car without being noticed? Without falling headlong onto the boards? Without being seriously injured? A tense feeling overcame me, and I considered pitching myself headlong onto the still ground, regardless of the after-effects.

Oh! That I had tried, even had all the harm in the world come upon me! Certainly, any fate would have been better than the one that is currently mine!

But then there was a terrific jolt and I pitched forward, grasping madly at the back of the seat facing me. I nearly flew over the whole seat, but the poles that supported the roof were my salvation, arresting my momentum and preventing me from falling headlong off of the car. Before I could recover my composure, however, a firm hand grasped my shoulder and I was being dragged off onto a concrete platform.

"What are you doing here?" a voice that was attached to the hand snarled in my ear. I turned uncomfortably and found myself looking up into the ugly face of a very tall man who appeared to be some type of security officer.

"I—I—I wanted to see—to see where they—where the tram cars go at night?" Certainly, there was no greater idiot of speech than I at that particular moment, but it did not seem to bother my attacker. Perhaps it was a small mercy that he did not choose to pummel me into senselessness right then, but perhaps he considered me stupid enough not to be deserving of his painful methods of punishment and simultaneously not stupid enough to be permitted a simple release.

His large hand still gripped my shoulder with painful accuracy. "Where the tram cars go at night?" he repeated my stammered question slowly, sneering down at me. "Well, here you are." Forcefully, he turned me about again so that I had to look around. "Take a look, buddy," he leered. "It may very well be the last thing you do!"

I immediately felt sickened and terrified, but I had no other recourse than to do his bidding and look about at the strange place that I was currently standing in.

It was a large bay, a type of garage that one would expect to see machinery in, but apparently only built in order to house the tram cars. It was covered, but mysteriously, there was one large window exactly in the center of the ceiling, a strange triangle-shaped window with ornate designs. I felt the fear ebbing away as I stepped forward to stare up at the window in fascination.

A shadow crossed my face and I jerked back in horror. Then I relaxed. There was only a scrawny young fellow standing before me who stared at me stoically.

Suddenly I recognized him and stammered out, "You—you drove—"

"I am Driver 52C, correct," he replied, calmly. His light blue eyes bored into mine and I determined that, though odd, he seemed like a nice enough fellow. Perhaps it would not turn out as badly as the pit in the middle of my stomach warned me that it could become. But oh! How wrong I was! Before I had a chance for my mind and my emotions to become reconciled, Driver 52C took my arm in a familiar way.

"Come on, it's time to take care of the tram voices."

"The—what?" I felt bewildered and shot a glance back at the towering security guard as he stood there, arms crossed, facing the door, standing directly under the window as if it was his to command who would look in or out, enter or depart, and conduct any other business in the strange garage.

"The tram voices," the young driver said conversationally in a nasally tone of voice. "Every night, the cars are brought in for inspection, and then, if our car passes inspection, we have a party— you know, music, food, drinks, games, fun stuff like that."

Immediately, I felt relief wash over me, but my mind settled upon one phrase. "But—but—what if—what if a tram car doesn't pass?" I wondered hesitantly.

He shrugged nonchalantly. "They pass. All the time." He gave me a slight push toward the wall. My eyes widened as I anticipated my face being crushed against the cement, but it would have been a small mercy had I then died from the impact. When my face was a mere two inches from the wall, it suddenly opened to reveal a smiling Asian girl standing in front of a spacious, well-lit room. Gaping, I walked in on the heels of Driver 52C, glancing back to see the silent door sliding shut behind us. And that girl—didn't I know her from somewhere? But no matter, it is of no importance.

And here, dear reader, is when my doom came about in the most hideous and horrible of ways. Steel yourself, I beg you, and if you have not nerves that match the strength of iron bars, I bid you an immediate and hasty farewell.

But alas, I must go on. Within the room, young people milled about casually, chatting lightly and carelessly, all of them appearing comfortable and at home, all of them wearing matching khaki pants or shorts and brightly colored shirts. Most of the shirts were yellow, but a few, like my driver's, wore bright teal. I assumed the colors designated rank in the tram car business, and my suspicion was confirmed when a young man in a black shirt approached.

My companion looked at him with a smile. "Hey, Boss."

"All set?" Mr. Black Shirt returned, a grin wreathing his face. He glanced at me once my driver nodded. "Welcome. Shirt size?"

I blinked, immediately feeling suspicious. "I don't work here," I said belligerently. Curse the day! Curse my foolishness! Had I but accepted the shirt with reverence, I would remain sane to this day!

But the young man merely raised his eyebrows casually and gave a nonchalant shrug, just like my driver had some moments earlier. "Then, I am sorry," he said, turning away. Suddenly, he turned back. "Are you certain?" he asked, glancing at me and then my driver. Was it my imagination, or did he appear slightly sympathetic?

Looking back, I consider him a generous benefactor who offered me a ray of hope in a world of doom. Curse my brash honesty! Curse my impatience! Curse my cruelty! Curse the day I ignored his kindness!

But I cannot undo the harsh truth, and I fully deserve where currently I dwell within my miserable state of mind. At this point, everything becomes a blur within my memory. I know that I glanced around the room, which was lined on all sides with equipment of some nature. But I saw no tram cars, and therefore I had not the faintest idea what those dreadful black boxes of mischief truly were. There was no food, there was no drink, and certainly, that should have clued me in to the fact that this would be the final day of doom in my short and wretched life.

"Drivers up," Mr. Black Shirt said casually and everyone immediately appeared alert. His dark eyes flashed toward me. "Welcome to our guest," he said, and this time, I was certain that he appeared sympathetic.

Bless his kindness toward me and curse the moment I reviled his mercy! And woe betide his cruel underlings who shared not his worthy sentiments! In that moment of impending doom, I faced a mocking ripple of laughter that drifted through the room, echoing about eerily as the sounds reflected against the mysterious black boxes of misery perched about that wretched room in which I lost myself, my true self. Day of horrors!

"Shall we begin?" the boss of the party asked, but the question sounded more like a command than anything else. The crowd of employees did not mind, apparently, for a quiet murmur of assent passed all around me and I straightened up in anticipation. God help me for forgetting to remain alert! Had I but guarded my mind and steeled my resolve against the horrors to come instead of letting down my guard, I am certain I could have lasted a while longer!

But I was tired and longed for some amusement. It had been a hard day, and a disappointing one as well. At that moment, I felt that this miserable adventure to discover where the tram cars returned to at night had turned out to be less than I hoped. An ordinary garage building with a weird window and a hostile guard, not to mention the peculiar gathering of staff. It was enough to make me want to wilt in frustration.

"Then all hail our illustrious chant, and let the celebration begin," Mr. Black Shirt's voice broke into my wretched thoughts.

Curse my curiosity! Curse my numb willingness to listen! Curse my lazy acceptance of what was to come! In my mind's eye, I still see the tram car drivers gathering in a large circle around me, their faces brightening, their postures lifting, as if a load had been removed from their backs or their minds. All their illumined faces turned toward Mr. Black Shirt as he broke from the circle and proceeded to the furthest wall, approaching those little black machines of misery and doom.

Ah! I cannot! I cannot go on! It is too much for my wretched mind! Curse them! Curse him! Curse me! Curse everything!

But I must, I must repeat this to the end, though it may very well be the very last thing that I ever do. And I shall, in penance for my laziness, my idiocy, my stupidity that has cost me a hundredfold today and for every day to come that is left in my wretched existence.

What miserable thing happened when the black-shirted tram car employee approached the wall? Quite simply, dear reader, he turned on a switch on one of those little pathetic machines. And what came out of that little speaker box? Surely you know!

"Watch the tram car, please," the automated voice announced.

Curse me! But I laughed when I heard it. It was a joke, I thought, and the crowd of idiots was part of it. Curse me! Curse me forever! The most wretched night of my life and I wasted my last laugh on that sick message!

But my misery was not complete. Mr. Black Shirt proceeded in a slow circle about the room, clicking the switch on each machine, one after another, on and on and on and on, without remorse or pity for my poor bewildered ears! The great circle of tram car drivers began to clap and cheer in delight, for the message of warning began to fill the room, echoing and re-echoing, becoming louder and louder, faster and faster! My doom approached with haste and swiftness! There must have been over one hundred of those terrible machines!

Instinctively, my hands went to my ears and I cringed, wanting to flee. Curse me! But there was nowhere to flee toward!

At that moment, the drivers all turned and grinned at me, and I felt my brain slowly and surely beginning to short-circuit. Dear reader, I cannot fully explain, for the horror and shock was complete. The only thing I am able to state for your understanding is that all the drivers had become transformed into monsters. Each person's eyes were flashing, yes, you heard that right—they were flashing red, yellow, green, blue, indeed, all the neon colors that I abhorred! Their faces were illumined to reflect and collect as much color as possible, and I feared that I would die on the spot.

Oh, that I had died! Oh, that I had perished in that moment! But alas, no one pitied me to kill me and relieve me of my misery! It was too much! To hear the tram car message repeated a thousand times over was one thing, but to be faced with the added tumult of colors and lights, I had reached the end!

Dear reader, I attempt to deal with this carefully and logically for your sake and for yours alone. I have indeed reached the end, but I pray that you will not be traumatized by the horror of my situation, even by hearing such a dreadful story. Looking back, the only thing that I can say at the end of this is that my whole being had reached the very end of wholeness and sanity. The only response I could offer in my frailty to this horrible evening was to scream in pain and misery. And indeed, that is what happened. A rising tide began to build somewhere in my stomach, and I thought I might get sick and vomit or lose my mind and faint. Then came forth a great and terrible scream from the center of my being that went on—and on—and on—

When I came to, I was half-lying, half-sitting in the sand against a concrete pillar underneath the boardwalk. Behold me in my deserted and miserable form, and pity me. Or not, for I fully deserve the wretched end I have finally come to. Shuddering, I struggled to my feet, brushing myself off, checking to make sure I was all there. Glancing around, I felt discomfited and lost but stumbled forward. I had not gone three steps before tripping over a body and landing face-first in the sand. It was a human body, I am certain, but I could not look back. I was insane, and I panicked. Yes, I struggled up and fled across the sand toward the seashore.

What happened all that morning, I cannot say. I vaguely remember running for a time, until sharp pains in my head and in my body forced me to rest. What I do know is that it was a miserable time, and was only a foretaste of what the remainder of my existence has been. Perhaps I shall die soon. What a blissful thought! It would be a welcome rest from my everlasting torment.

Oh, reader, the days and nights have become unimaginable. You cannot think how it is to be worthless and meaningless because of the trauma one has faced in a single night. Just think! A solitary event can shatter the mind, the soul, the body, the spirit—all of the being so horribly and totally as to render life utterly pointless. I cannot talk about it any further.

There is only one last thing I shall say before departing in my haze of doom and allowing you to return to your normal and happy life. It is my vague memory of when I finally returned from the beach to the boardwalk and forced myself to return to my hotel and then prepare to go home.

Home? What is that? I cannot say, for the concept of home is also meaningless, but I digress.

I was on the beach, faint with the heat, with exhaustion, with thirst, with hunger. I had no concept of time or space, for my mental capacity was diminished to some negligible and unquantifiable amount. The only thing I knew was that it was time to leave the miserable stretch of sand and consider taking care of my wasted body in a more appropriate setting.

Once I reached the boardwalk, all of the horrible memories came flashing back—the tram car, the guard in the garage, the driver with the black shirt, the circle of people surrounding me, the endless horror of the miserable tram car message. Had all of that really happened? Or had it all been a dream? Staggering away from the wilderness of sand, I grasped the railing and stumbled up the steps. It smelled like the early morning and as my feet hit the first boards, I felt warmth, unexpectedly, and turned back, instinctively.

The sun was rising across the sky away from the ocean, and the beauty of it caused me to sigh in relief. Whatever had happened was finally over. I was alive and well, even though I was starving and disoriented. Taking a deep breath, I turned and began walking down the boards toward the end of the line.

Hearing a creaking sound behind me, I turned and saw the tram car coming up on my left. I started violently, and reality caught me in its cold clutches.

Dear reader, you can never imagine the horror of that moment. It was nearly as bad as waking up to the morning on the sandy shore and forcing myself to remember the nightmares of that miserable evening. To be given hope so suddenly and have it forcibly removed was an experience I shall never recover from. But I must avoid sounding too melodramatic. Reality is awful at times, and this was one of those events. It cannot be lessened, and it must not be exaggerated. In this case, it destroyed my tenuous hope, and that was the end of the glory of the morning. To this day, I have never looked at the world with delight.

But I digress once again. I was back on the boardwalk, forcing myself to control my wobbling knees and quivering emotions. I refused to bolt and run, to lose the last vestige of my humanity, no matter how much of it had already been forcibly removed from me. So I acted in any way that an insane man might, pretending with the last energy within me that I was truly normal. Swallowing hard, I shoved my hands in my pockets and hunched my shoulders, repeating to myself in my head over and over and over again. "It is a dream. It is a dream. It is a dream. It is a dream."

The creaking stopped and I heard a voice. Well, as I came to realize, it was my own.

"It is a dream."

I opened my eyes and to my disgust, I was looking at the tram car, which most definitely was not a dream. Surrendering myself to the inevitable horror that my reality now consisted of, I looked at the driver and found a familiar face.

Yes, it was Driver 52C, as usual.

He grinned at me. "Beautiful day!"

Curse him! What a wretch! I said nothing in reply but stared at him with what I hoped was a blank stare. More likely, it was an angry gape, but may all the curses rest upon him and his devious ways.

He grinned again, too familiarly, I felt. "Heading down to the end?"

"Yeah, the Crest," I replied, feeling all my bitterness, anger, and frustration mounting. I wished to tear him to pieces. I knew for certain that my teeth would sprout into wolf's fangs and my fingernails into lion's claws, were I but given a chance to have at him. But he was speaking again.

"Want a ride?" With yet another obnoxious grin, he added, "On the house."

"No!" I exploded and turned away from him as I marched off, woodenly, my rage complete. I heard his mocking voice behind me as I stumbled on mechanically.

"Well, as they say, 'Watch the tram car, please.'" His voice was teasing, but fortunately for him, he resisted pressing the evil button and playing the freaky recorded message. Otherwise, I truly would have torn him into bits.

Where did all this rage come from? Surely, it is from my insanity and I do not ask for any pity or sympathy. I only ask that, now, as my tragic tale comes to a dismal end, that you quietly leave for your own pretty life and that you heed my bitter advice, as I am deserted to die in my doom, that you, O reader, never ask that fatal question, "Where do the tram cars go at night?"

That is all.

9
We're All Going to Die

As told by Nathan Levy

I glanced at my watch and shuddered. It was a quarter to the hour, and I was not prepared for all hell to break loose. I heard it from the neighbors, and the incessant village alarms reminded me of the disaster to come.

The whole house was in disarray. The couple I had been staying with for the past week were already gone. The adults were smart. They left at the first sign of danger. We had stayed behind—reckless or bold—call it what you wish.

My friends, the two older children, and their two friends were hastily packing—disorderly, panicked. Trouble was coming, and swift action was required.

I had not quite reached the state of panic. I was in more of a daze. Everything felt blurry and surreal. I stood there at the kitchen counter, placing non-perishable foods into a backpack. I felt like I was moving too slowly, but there was nothing I could do to hasten my actions. I needed food, water, extra clothing, and more ammunition for my weapon.

"Ten minutes!" one of the girls screamed, rushing from the kitchen toward the backdoor.

I gulped.

Suddenly, I did not care about food. I did not want to be in the house when the enemy reached the village. I did not want to be anywhere near the village when the houses were being razed to the ground. I had no emotional attachment to the area, but it was the utter destruction of humanity that terrified me.

Food would only slow me down. I threw the backpack over my shoulder and headed for the bedroom. I already had some clothes set aside. It would only take a moment to throw them in the backpack. All my other equipment was neatly packed, I just needed an extra box of ammunition. It was under the bed. I leaned down and stuck my hand under the bed to retrieve it.

Another scream from one of the girls sent a wave of shock into me, and I threw myself face down on the floor. Gasping from the jolt of adrenaline that pulsed through my veins, I forced myself up on my hands and knees. Obviously, the daze was gone. The panic was beginning to set in.

I shoved the ammo into the backpack and zipped it shut. Standing up, I jerked back the blankets on the bed and pushed the pillow aside, taking the gun from the place it always rested until I left the house in the morning. The papers. I gulped and picked them up, too.

Last week, I had been at my grandmother's house.

I could still see her, standing there on the porch that always reminded me of a tropical greenhouse. She had heard of the alarm and was leaving. She pressed her documentation and identification forms into my shaking hands, telling me that she would be searched on her way out of the country and could not be found alive or dead with them. I took them reluctantly, feeling a chill. I was loyal to the point of my own death, but it was a death sentence to be a courier.

Most people burned their papers, but others hoped to be able to reenter the fatherland and hid them.

My sister arrived just as my grandmother was leaving. She had driven her gray jeep into the lot, ripped off the plates, and threw them into the river. I remembered the way her gray eyes lit up when she saw me. We had not seen each other for weeks. She had given me her papers as well and asked about the rest of the family.

All I had been able to tell her was that they were in my backpack. My father had asked me to take all the younger siblings' forms. His own papers—and those of my mother—he had burned. Of course, I had my own papers. I felt like I was carrying peoples' souls with me. I was not only one person. I was eight people in one. If the enemy caught me—

I stopped myself and snapped back into reality. It was no time to dream or reminisce. They could not catch me. Even if I were to be killed to avoid torture, it would mean the capture of my loved ones. I must hide the papers.

Before I could think of an adequate way to hide or pack them, the alarm sounded more urgently from the village hall. Then the sound of an explosion.

It was time.

I shoved the plastic-wrapped package into the front pocket of my backpack, forced the handgun into my concealed holster, and turned toward the side porch. In my mind's eye, I could see the heavily armed enemy approach the front door with a drawn weapon, force the remaining girl to open the door, and let him in to search the house. There was nothing I could do to help my friends. There was nothing I could do to stop him. I could hear it. They were already storming the village.

The numbness was gone. Everything was crystal clear. I was going to die—one way or another—and the papers would be found. There was nothing I could do except try to delay the inevitable for a few minutes longer. I had waited too long.

Slipping to the side door, I looked out to the adjacent house. The occupants were walking out with their hands raised, their faces blank, automatons in motion. Like me, they had resigned themselves to the inevitable and ceased to care. I counted. Three, four, five—the people kept coming from the house. Then I remembered there were about ten of them. Time for me to leave before the guard followed the last prisoner from the house. I slipped out the door, rounded the side of the house, and ducked down nervously behind the chest-high bushes.

The road was in front of me. Vehicles from the enemy convoy were parked helter-skelter along the shoulders. It seemed so disorganized, and I began reorganizing them in my mind, but then I realized the situation was perfect. Their disorganization gave me an advantage.

I glanced toward the line of prisoners walking down the driveway toward the road. I caught the eye of one girl. She had tossed her head back to swing the straight blonde hair out of her sharp green eyes. She nodded slightly at me, and I realized what she was telling me. I was safe for the moment if I remained where I was. I nodded back, slightly, feeling helpless that I could not give her some encouragement in return.

I still heard the enemy crashing inside the house I just vacated. Then the door from my bedroom burst open, and one of the young men exited, followed by his sister. They looked at me, desperately, two pairs of blue eyes meeting a pair of dark brown eyes in one critical moment.

Now it was my chance. The enemy would be exiting the same door. If I reentered the house from the kitchen door, I would be safe for a few more critical moments. I turned to dash up the stairs, but a cry made me halt in my tracks.

There—down the driveway about forty yards away—a group of prisoners were facing an armed guard, caught in uncertainty as they stood poised to flee. I wanted to tell them to stop, not to be foolish. They would be mowed down by the machine guns like corn facing a harvester.

But then—I saw the blonde-haired girl look desperately in my direction. I glanced at the guard. His gaze was fixedly marked on a tall young man who looked like trouble. I nodded at her, and she fled in my direction, causing the others around her to also flee in opposite directions.

A babble of confused voices and cries filled the air. Then the angry sounds of the enemy calling for a halt to the madness met my ears. Behind me, the kitchen door burst open, and I started violently, fleeing toward the group. I felt like a caribou hunted by wolves and wished to hide myself inside the herd so I would not be singled out for a meal.

More angry shouts along with the metallic sounds of guns, and I knew that the next noise we would all hear would be bullets tearing through the air and—if we were doomed—then meet eternal silence.

I threw myself down on the ground instinctively, letting my body roll to the side, my face turned back toward the house, just as the ugly rat-tat-tat began. I closed my eyes and wished I had the ability to close my ears as I heard the sickening sound of bullets ripping through living flesh and the terrified screams of the wounded.

A body fell across my torso, causing a black shadow to come between my shut eyes and the bright mid-day sun. I could tell by the way they fell that they would never rise again. I blinked once, twice, then shut my eyes again with a sick feeling in my stomach when I saw blonde hair and red splotches on the gravel beside my head.

The shooting ceased, and I lay perfectly still with minimal breathing. After a minute, I opened my eyes, forcing myself not to focus on the corpse that still rested heavily against me. I heard footsteps, and my eyelids drifted to half-mast as I allowed my body to completely relax. I hoped that my pounding heart was not audible.

An eternity later, the only sound I heard was distant voices and motors. Then flies began to buzz, and the birds resumed their singing in the trees. I felt a lump beginning to form in my throat. Why was reality so cruel that wherever death was, life still remained present? Why didn't everything shrivel up and die in the sight of such gross and repulsive murder? Why must the living continue to breathe and function normally?

At the thought of that, I silently willed myself to die. I thought of standing up and shouting, calling attention to myself so that I would be put out of my misery. But yet—death still remained repulsive. There was nothing in it that would cause me to desire it for myself. I still craved existence.

To live! To breathe! To exist!

I sighed and then caught myself. The slightest motion could mean the end of my life. With that, I resigned myself to motionlessness.

My back already hurt—the backpack digging into my twisted shoulders in a most unkind manner. The handgun ground into my lower back. The gravel pierced my bare left arm and the side of my head where I had landed heavily on the ground. The flies buzzed about my face, thinking I was one of the dead.

Agony.

Pain.

Torture.

I opened my eyes from the living hell to the sound of revved-up motors that became louder and then gradually began to fade. Along with it, the faint sounds of wailing, weeping, and gnashing of teeth. I wondered if the latter was my imagination, for then silence reigned.

I waited with a clenched jaw, counting slowly to one thousand. I was tempted to stop at one hundred but did not dare. I counted one hundred for each of the souls I represented, and then two hundred for the poor dead girl resting against the painful hollow between my ribcage and my pelvis.

The sun now hung lower in the sky. I blew the flies from my face and then slowly struggled to rise, glancing about cautiously to distract myself from the agony of summoning my body to function after having remained still for so long.

The pain was kind to me. I admit that it was a welcome agony, for it reminded me that I was alive.

I struggled upward, reaching toward the blue sky above and the bright yellow sun that smiled downward. I stopped on my hands and knees, squinting about awkwardly, wanting to vomit. I swallowed hard, the dryness in my mouth reminding me of the first time I tried to eat a persimmon, not knowing that it was not completely ripe.

Why this pleasant and humorous memory despite the wretchedness all around me?

I halted in my crawl back toward the house, hearing a vehicle. I threw myself down on my side, wincing as sore muscles were tortured once again. I waited for the truck to stop, for the enemy to surround me, and pummel me until I gave up the souls I held onto tightly.

I wanted to laugh aloud at the irony. My body already ached. They could not do anything to me that I had already not felt.

But the truck passed, and I struggled upward again. I would hide under the kitchen porch until nightfall and then make for the woods behind the development. If I followed the stream upwards, it would lead me to safety. As long as I could find the friendly forces within a week, I could survive on my own.

Creeping under the porch, I glanced backward at the bodies still lying in the hot sun. It was a shame to leave them there. I thought about nightfall, wishing I could find a shovel and could bury each one of them in the light of the moon.

A stubborn thought came into my mind. Leave them there. Let them rot in the sun. Let the bodies decay and fill the air with a stench that any passerby would not soon forget. Let the country remember how evil the enemy is. Let the world see how ugly murder and destruction are.

I felt wetness on my hand as I knelt there. I glanced down. Water. Eagerly, I lifted my hand to my face and tasted it. Saltwater? I touched my face and was surprised to find tears on my cheeks.

No matter, I told myself. It was all right to cry, even if I did not have time to. I turned and crawled under the porch. I curled myself into a tight ball, closing my eyes to the world.

Oh, you cruel old world, how I hate you.

I sighed and ignored the feeling of suppressed grief. I had no time to mourn. I had not seen the whole of ugliness. I still had a mission.

I felt something on my hand and opened my eyes. Raising my hand to eye level, I saw a small inchworm crawling across my thumb. It was so tiny. It must have hatched only days ago.

I sighed. Why was it that there was always life where death was also present? Why must life go on when death has already swallowed those who wished to remain on earth?

I wanted to crush that stupid baby inchworm into nonexistence. He had no right to begin to live when I was facing death.

But what right had I to be alive when a good number of my friends had just walked into the yawning mouth of eternity? Why was I here without a scratch on me when the others had been sacrificed by the bullets pointed in my direction?

I gently flicked the worm away, wiping the silk off my hand and folding my hands underneath my aching head once more.

Be silent, my brain, I commanded myself, closing my eyes tightly. I felt suddenly weary and tried to ignore it by popping my eyelids back open. I had too many things to think about and to plan for. I had a dangerous journey ahead. I could not sleep on the job now. I had to watch and wait until nightfall.

I yawned and blinked furiously. Why was I so tired? I was terribly thirsty. I felt weak.

As soon as dusk fell, I would rise from my hiding place and attend to my immediate needs. Then, I would head across the short plain toward the woods, the safety of the mountain ranges with their flowing streams, into friendly territory—

My eyelids drifted shut as sleep sucked me into its inescapable vortex.

10
One Curious Night

As told by Elsie Thompson

I was washing dishes in the back when Jane Prins came in and jerked me away from the sink. She started babbling something at me about some woman needing me somewhere, as she shoved a dry towel into my dripping hands and began untying my apron. I was used to being manhandled by this tank of a person, but I hoped desperately that I was not being forced into the lineup of women sold out for the night.

After inspecting my clothes, Jane ordered me to go change and be ready to leave in five minutes. "Wear something nice," she snapped at me, glaring at my back as I began to walk away. She knew that my definition of nice was too conservative for her liking, but what could I say?

Going up the stairs quickly, I went into the small room I shared with a couple of other women, put on a clean shirt and skirt, and then put on some socks and shoes. Most of the time here, I went barefoot, even though it was supposedly against regulations. Who was to care? Most women were too poor to own shoes.

I went to the dingy window and looked out, seeing my reflection despite the grime. I redid my hair quickly and then sighed, not prepared to face the unknown of the night. Turning back to the doorway, I took a light jacket as an afterthought. It was not cold, but the nights could be cool, and I did not know where I was going.

Jane Prins was in the dining room. I stood in the doorway, waiting for her to notice me. She was talking to a woman who was expensively dressed and held the stem of a wine glass between gloved fingertips. Jane's hands and arms flew around expansively, and then she tapped her foot, looking back at the doorway and seeing me. Waving her hands impatiently, she jerked her head in my direction.

Meekly, I went toward them, avoiding several tables at which men and scantily-clad women sat, sipping on alcohol and snacking on dainties. I noticed several glances in my direction but ignored them all.

I stood there in front of the table, allowing the woman to inspect me. She had a lot of makeup on and appeared frazzled. Perhaps the wine was her attempt to calm herself. After a few seconds, she turned back to Jane and spoke in an austere smoker's voice.

"She's not much to look at."

Jane laughed, her voice without humor. "How right you are. She has no sense of style and refuses to wear anything except what sort of rags she has on. But she is a hard worker, and honest, and you will never find a bad thing about her. I've had her for five years, and she has not caused me any trouble."

"None at all?" the woman said dubiously.

"None at all," Jane said stolidly.

Suddenly, the woman looked in my direction, her face crafty. "Honest, eh? Have you ever caused Jane any trouble?"

I smiled slightly, unable to help myself. "Yes, I constantly annoy her, though she is definitely getting better at handling my eccentricities."

"Well, I—!" Mrs. Prins burst out, shocked and horrified, and then she subsided with a nervous titter.

The woman seemed pleased and amused. Sitting back in her chair with a much more relaxed appearance, she studied my face. I was no longer smiling, but I felt as if the humor was not gone for the evening.

"Do tell more," she said, raising a gloved hand toward me.

"There is not much more to tell," I replied evenly. "I have a certain code of ethics that prevents me from doing the sort of things that the other women under Mrs. Prins's direction have no trouble doing."

"Such as?" the woman said narrowly.

I paused, and then glanced around the room, slightly motioning to the other people present. "I do not give favors to men, or women for that matter," I added, noticing one booth in which three women sat together, obviously not only intending to enjoy one another's conversation.

Returning my eyes to the woman's face, I concluded, "I am here to work, and I am not interested in wasting time or energy on anything else."

The woman seemed taken aback. She looked at Jane, who was obviously embarrassed but said nothing for once. "How quaint," she finally said, sipping at her wine. Setting down the glass definitively, she rose. "I'll take her."

Mrs. Prins was recovered. She also rose and began talking business. I had heard it before, so I let it fade into the background as I focused on keeping myself calm.

Presently, I found myself following the woman outside the building to a limousine. She waved me in ahead of herself and then sat by the window, the driver closing the door behind us. I sat quietly and said nothing, fully expecting the woman to make some sort of introduction and offer an explanation of what duty lay ahead.

But nothing came. The whole drive we sat in silence. I have no idea how long the drive took, but it seemed like an eternity. After several minutes wasted in worry, I began daydreaming of other things.

The car slowed and came to a stop. The driver got out and opened the side door, the one closer to me. I glanced at the silent woman, and she waved me out. A bit confused and nervous, I exited and then watched as the driver walked back around the vehicle and got back in. I stood there and watched in confusion as they drove away. I did not know what to think. Before I could collect my scattered thoughts, someone shouted at me.

I turned. A middle-aged man was standing on the porch of a house surrounded by trees, shouting profanities after the car. It was ironic, even though I felt afraid of him and the new situation, I thought that he summed up the situation perfectly. Unfortunately, I cannot reproduce his explanation of the situation, since he was so vulgar that I had to shut my ears to it instead of trying to redeem what he was screaming.

Presently, he calmed. He stared at me. Finally, he spoke in a normal voice. "Well, come in."

Obediently, I followed him up the stairs into the house. It was an expensive place, but it was a mess. Not so much dirty as cluttered with random belongings, mostly children's toys and clothing, it appeared. My assumption was correct, for as we entered the large living area, I caught sight of three children fighting in the middle of the floor.

"Cut it out!" the man yelled at them, and then he turned to me, staring at me for a moment.

Finally, he spoke. "I'm Peter. Those are the kids you're supposed to wash up and put to bed. They ate supper already. I was supposed to go out with that woman but obviously, she has other plans for tonight." He sat down at a nearby raised counter on a bar stool. "I need a drink," he said with a sigh. "After you're finished with the kids, get me a pack of whiskey from the basement."

"Okay," I replied, at a loss. A pack of whiskey? Put the kids to bed? I glanced back at him, but he was lost in the recesses of his own mind, doodling on the counter, pushing some crumbs around that appeared as if they had fallen off of a large plate of sandwiches.

There was a lot to figure out, but the kids were clamoring again. There were three of them, a girl and a boy that looked like twins, around five, and the other was a younger girl. Taking a deep breath, I went over toward them and bent down.

They stopped squabbling and looked at me sullenly, but expectantly.

"Hi," I said, smiling slightly. They were cute kids, even though I could tell they were spoiled brats. "Guess what time it is?"

The boy looked up at a nearby clock and shrugged. His twin sister held up her grimy hand that had remnants of supper on it.

"Five," she replied.

The toddler laughed.

"No, it's bedtime," I replied, fully expecting a barrage of crying and anger.

To my surprise, they looked at one another, laughed, and returned to their toys. I waited a second, puzzled. I was going to repeat myself when the little boy looked at me.

"What's bedtime?"

"It is when you go to sleep in the night."

They all looked bewildered, but I felt bewildered. Then they laughed and went back to their toys again.

I stood up. Either they were dimwits or I was losing it. "Well, come on," I said, leaning down and picking up the fat little girl. She appeared as if she had not had a bath or a change in quite a long time. She did not fight me. In fact, she seemed happy to be picked up by a complete stranger.

I was feeling odder and odder about this situation. But the twins got up and followed me—to where?

"Where is your room?" I asked.

"Upstairs," said the boy.

"Okay, let's go," I said with relief.

We went up an expensive staircase. "That is my room," a boy said, pointing straight ahead. "That is Tessie's room," he said, pointing to the right. "And that is Bubbie's room," he said, pointing to the left."

All of the rooms were enormous, and I did not know where to start. But the last room appeared least threatening. The Boy Room had too much blue and orange. The Tessie Room was too pink and purple. The Bubbie Room seemed a bit more subdued, even though it had bottles and pacifiers painted onto the trim. So, I led the way and we all went in.

"How about a bath?" I suggested.

They all looked at me dumbly.

"Okay, a bath it is," I said, heading toward the two doors on the side. The first was a closet, and they all laughed. I laughed also, though I stopped for a moment to admire the rows and rows of children's clothing. It appeared that Bubbie was set for life.

The second doorway led to an enormous bathroom. I set the bath water running and stripped all the kids, putting them all into the gigantic bathtub and adding plenty of bubbles. I was met with very little resistance. In fact, they all seemed amazed and delighted. It became obvious after a while that they were neglected, and it made me infuriated.

So, the kiddies had a bath for a while, and I took a bit of time to snoop through the ginormous closet and pick out bedtime clothes for all of them. I checked the bed, also, which was very large, and appeared that it had not been slept in for quite a while. But it was clean, and I decided to put them all in the same bed.

Returning to the bathroom, they were all having fun, but the littlest one appeared tired, so I drained the tub, rinsed and dried them all off, and helped them on with the diapers and pajamas. Again, the amazement and compliance. It was so peculiar.

By the time they got into the big bed, they were falling over themselves with weariness. I began to wonder when the last time was that they had a normal bedtime and sleep schedule. I fully intended to tell them a story, but by the time I covered them up, they were all fast asleep.

Puzzled, I straightened and looked down at their peacefully sleeping faces. After a moment, I cleaned up the room and the bathroom and then headed downstairs to see what other odd things would come to pass.

The man, their father I assumed, was still sitting in the kitchen. He raised his head. "How about my pack of whiskey?"

"Of course," I murmured, and then headed for the doorway, instinct guiding me back to the messy laundry room and a side door that led downstairs.

There was a very large family room down there, and a back area with appliances, utilities, and random things. There was also a large amount of alcohol. And, strangest of all, there was also this thing that I had never seen before—whiskey in six packs. Yes, whiskey in cans. I picked up a case and brought it upstairs.

Peter took the whiskey and retreated to a corner of the living room, flicking on the TV as he went. I stared at him for a moment, sighed, and then began to pick up the toys scattered around the first floor of the house.

It was an odd night and the mysteries continued to grow. Everything in the house was extravagant, and some things could not be explained. What was wrong with the kids? What was wrong with Peter? Who was the strange woman, and where did she go? How were they so rich but so miserable? Why was there so much food in platters all over the kitchen? Odd indeed.

After everything was clean, I stood in the living room and stared out the big picture window. It was a great view of the surrounding woods. It was not completely dark out, for the moon was very bright. Everything sparkled, as if it was wet or as if snow had fallen, even though it did not snow in these regions until much later in winter.

As I watched, I saw something amazing and astonishing. A tremendous herd of deer appeared as out of a fine mist and began running across the woods from the left. They ran as if terrified, and suddenly another herd of deer began running from the right and nearly collided with the first herd. They converged and seemed to gather energy from each other, and then the whole group began running toward the left, the first herd whirling about to go in the direction that the second herd was originally running toward.

It did not make any sense, but after a moment, I saw great shadows coming after the disappearing deer herd. I stepped forward, straining my eyes. Could it be? It was ridiculous, but I was certain. A buffalo and a bull moose were chasing the deer herd, and a hundred yards behind the males, their females also ran. The animals went on and on until they disappeared into the woods far to the left.

Before I could relax from that excitement, I saw other shadows coming, this time directly away from the house. These shadows appeared humanoid, and they were numerous, though not as many as the deer. There were at least twenty. They came closer, and I recognized them as soldiers.

"Mr. Peter," I said, turning around to face him. I had to call him again to get his attention away from the TV. "There are soldiers coming."

He nodded, as if bored. "The food is for them," he said, motioning to the kitchen and reaching for another can of whiskey.

I glanced back at the slowly approaching infantry men, and then took in a deep breath. Obviously, it was up to me. Turning, I began uncovering all the plates of food and arranging them quickly on the kitchen counters, buffet style. They could eat at the enormous table, at the kitchen bar, or where they pleased. I dearly hoped that they would not catch the sight of the alcohol. If there was one thing that disgusted and horrified me, it was a group of men and free-flowing alcohol.

Before I felt adequately prepared, there was a rap at the door, and then it opened of its own volition. I turned, towel in hand. A lieutenant stood in the doorway, staring at me as if in shock. I felt immediately uncomfortable. Did I appear that out of place in this strange house?

But the soldier recovered himself. "Ma'am," he said, removing his cap respectfully.

I nodded in acknowledgment and stepped aside, motioning to the food, the rest being self-explanatory. I stood there and watched as they filed in, washing up at the sink and then taking up plates and silverware before loading up their plates and sitting down at the nearby seats to eat. They were not loud, but there were twenty-three of them, I counted, and it created a dull sort of roar in the house.

I desperately hoped that the kids would be able to sleep well in the midst of the noise. Still, I stood there with the towel in my hand, waiting, keeping an eye on everything. At last, the lieutenant went through the line and came to stand beside me with his plate of food and glass of water in his hands. The table was full and some of the soldiers had wandered to the living room, but the bar was open.

"Sir, would you like to sit down?" I asked, feeling uneasy.

He put the glass away from his lips. "Ah, yes, thank you, ma'am." He walked over to the bar and sat, then looked back at me, as if he expected me to follow. Taking a deep breath, I dutifully went and stood nearby.

"Have a seat, ma'am," he said, tucking into his plate.

I obeyed, not knowing why I did. There were things to clean up, but I waited patiently.

The lieutenant swallowed and looked at me. "You the housekeeper here?"

"No, sir."

His fork stopped in midair, and he asked, "Then who are you, and what are you, and why are you here?"

I restrained a smile. Even though I did not like male attention, I liked his straightforward attitude. "I work at the Olde Tavern in Middletown, and I was hired out for tonight to help over here."

He interrupted me with a grunt. "Trashy place. What's a nice girl like you doing there?" Then before I had a chance to answer, he straightened. "You don't even look like the type. So, what's the deal?"

"I was not given a choice in the matter," I replied calmly.

"Oh, right," he said as if there was no more discussion needed. He ate on for a while, and I did not find it necessary to say anything else. Then he put down his fork, glanced at me, looked around the room, and settled his gaze on me again.

"Look, I can help you out," he said in a lowered tone.

I looked at him evenly, a bit curious about what he had to say, but I was not expecting much.

"That drunken sod over in the corner isn't going to protest if we march you out of here. I have friends who could ship you out of the region, get you out west or something where the oppression isn't so intense."

I was touched by the suggestion, but I was not impressed. "Why should I leave?" I wondered. "I have plenty of work to do, and there are people who I am able to help on a regular basis. Who can say if I have been chosen to be here for such a time as this?"

He grunted and went back to his food for a few minutes. Then he raised his head and looked at me candidly. His attitude seemed somewhat changed. "I know you," he said quietly.

I shrugged, not recognizing him at all, fully expecting him to say something else ridiculous.

"I was good friends with Tom B— and his family. I worked with him. He was my chaplain back in Palestine. I recognize you from his group of workers."

At that, my face flushed. It had been so long since I had heard of those names and places and it made me want to go back to those days of busy work. I sighed but steeled my resolve.

"That's very kind of you, whoever you are, but I still have to stay here."

"I could kidnap you," he said suddenly.

I looked at him and then laughed, the irony of the situation hitting me full in the face. Finally, I shook my head. "Why would you do that?"

His voice was even lower than before. "What if I said that we needed you out west?"

"We?" I said skeptically, not buying it, even though I no longer felt nervous around him because of our shared friends.

He leaned toward me and unexpectedly put his hand on my arm. "There is a plan for an underground group," he said in a whisper. "I cannot speak of it here, but we need all the able-bodied and sound-minded citizens we can find."

"And what about yourself?" I asked, shaking his hand away.

He scraped his plate and forked the last bit of food into his mouth. "I'm a spy."

"I don't buy it," I said, my rage suddenly mounting. "You can lead part of the army and do any number of atrocious actions against helpless people and then say that you are actually helping the country?"

"I know it sounds bad, but this area—you have to believe me—the politics are so terrible that we are immobilized. We don't do anything except act like a general nuisance. And in the meantime, I lead my men while I gather and pass on information to Tom and his friends."

I rose and walked away from him, beginning to clean up the kitchen. I noticed that most of the soldiers were sprawling out in the living room and that while they had noticed the whiskey, they were not doing anything about it. I wondered if, perhaps, this lieutenant was telling the truth, and that his platoon was different because of his good leadership.

Well, I knew he was telling the truth, but I was unconvinced that my assistance was needed out west. It seemed cowardly to run away now when I had just begun to win the confidence of some of the women at the Tavern and begun to make a positive impact on their lives. Or, was it actually cowardly to stay? What did I really want to do? Or, more importantly, what was I supposed to do?

I turned back and glanced at the lieutenant still sitting at the bar. He was still watching me, and that made me feel annoyed. But I had a hunch that his sudden invitation did not come out of the blue. I had to know, and I had to ask.

Picking up some plates on my way over to him to make it appear casual, I leaned over and picked up his plate as I asked, "How long have you been looking for me?"

He smiled a bit sheepishly and then admitted, "Two months."

I straightened and looked up at him sternly. "And how did you know I would be here tonight?"

"I didn't," he replied. "Honest. I found out only recently that you were at the Tavern, and the plan was to hit there Friday night, but we've come here the past two Tuesdays, and here you are." He smiled again, genuinely this time. "I think it is fate."

"Fate," I repeated, still skeptical. Then I sighed and turned away, my hands now full of plates. I began to load the enormous dishwasher when he appeared with more plates. I straightened and looked at him head-on.

"What if I were to become a spy as well?" I asked, the idea suddenly coming to my mind.

He shook his head quickly, glanced around, and then stooped down, loading the dishwasher between his next words. "It is too dangerous for you. It is dangerous for me, but I am a soldier. You are a woman. No woman is safe these days, especially not a pretty young woman who is bold."

"Pretty young woman," I said in disgust. "You flatter me too much. I'm probably older than you."

He looked up at me with interest. "How old are you?"

"Forget it," I said sharply, but I had to laugh all the same.

"How is it," he wondered, seriously, "that you have survived so long without being seriously abused?"

I shrugged, thinking of all that I had seen, heard, and experienced in the last several years. What the lieutenant did not know would not hurt him, so I left the unknown dangling in the silence.

Finally, I said, "It is a dangerous world, yes, and I know that well."

Perhaps leaving it all a mystery was a mistake, for I could see in his eyes that his resolve to get me out west away from the immediate danger had been strengthened.

He stood up and leaned over the sink, his muscular hands gripping the sides of the counter and his forearms bulging. He stared across the room at his men and the TV as he spoke.

"Listen, I cannot explain everything to you here, but if you do not come with me willingly, I will kidnap you. We are all in agreement that you are more useful out there than here."

He turned to look at me. "Think honestly. What do you have here that is keeping you from going out west to live in freedom and security instead of being in daily dread of your life? What is it about your work at the Tavern that you like more than the idea of being with other like-minded people, able to work among them and help them instead of those who don't care if you live or die?"

I was taken aback. His questions were startling in a way that I did not expect. My face was still, but sudden tears sprang to my eyes and I instantly knew that my job here was done. It was time to be back with the people whom I truly loved and needed.

I think the soldier was surprised to see me crying. But he did not say anything else or try to convince me further since he could tell that his words had made their intended point. Reaching over, he picked up a napkin and handed it to me. When I did not take it, he tried to dab at the tears on my cheeks.

Drawing back, I looked at him full in the face, though he appeared blurry. When he said nothing more, I blinked the tears from my eyes and reached over past him. I picked up a dishcloth from the soapy water and squeezed it out on the side of the sink. I began wiping down the table and counters. By the time I returned to the sink, my tears were dried and my resolve was made.

The lieutenant looked at me, a bit tentatively but curiously. "Well? Am I going to have to kidnap you, or are you ready to leave?" He glanced at his watch. "We head out in one minute."

I took a deep breath and dropped the washcloth into the sink. "Let me wash my hands and turn on the dishwasher and I'll be ready to go."

11
Shelby's Wonderful Idea

A Holiday Tail, Part I

As told through the eyes of three special canines

It was two weeks before Christmas Day and Shelby had an idea. This was not that unusual, but for once, her idea had nothing to do with rubber balls, tennis balls, squeaky toys, or any other type of plaything that she adored.

Shelby bounded over to where Bailey was snoozing and nearly landed on top of her.

Bailey looked up groggily and yawned.

"Wake up! Wake up!" Shelby said, all excited.

"What is it?" Bailey asked in a patient, motherly tone.

"We need to buy a present for the boys!"

Simon turned from staring at a dead beetle in the corner of the room. "The boys?" he said critically.

"I think she means the human boys," Bailey said quietly, watching Shelby dash around the room in excitement.

"Yes, yes, the human boys, the tall ones," Shelby said, panting from her sudden workout. "We will surprise them. It will be amazing!"

"And how do you intend to do that, pray tell?" Simon asked in a supercilious tone, rising from his seat and walking over arrogantly. "Who is going to sell anything to a ditzy puppy dog? Please do inform me. Or do you intend to commit theft or grand larceny? Seriously, have you even thought this through, you idiot?"

"Simon, Simon," Bailey reprimanded quietly, but Shelby was undeterred. Jumping over to Simon, she nipped him playfully, causing him to turn on her angrily.

"Will you desist!" he said furiously, but she only laughed.

"You will do it for us, Mr. Genius!" Shelby said happily, "Just wait and see!" Then she went rushing out of the room.

"You shouldn't be so harsh to her," Bailey said in a disapproving tone to Simon after the golden hurricane had disappeared around the corner.

"She is extremely frustrating!" Simon replied bitterly. "You cannot comprehend the manner in which she causes me great vexation and sorrow because of her behavior!"

"I wouldn't be concerned if I were you," Bailey said sarcastically. "You give plenty of clues about how you feel. But, she is an affectionate puppy, and she does not have a mean hair on her. In fact, she rather likes you, so the least you can do is say a few kind words to her now and then, even if her ideas are silly."

Sulkily, Simon went back to his beetle in the corner and turned his back on the older female. "You would not understand," he said in a grumpy voice. "Just forget it."

At that instant, Shelby appeared from the adjoining room, guilt written all over her face and her tail wagging furiously. Before Bailey could ask what she had done, Shelby trotted over and deposited The Man's phone in front of Bailey's nose.

"What is this, dear?" Bailey asked, a bit of mild anxiety entering her tone. "Are you trying to get me in trouble?"

"Amazon! Amazon!" Shelby said in excitement, beginning to run around the room again. "I have the best gift ever!" Returning to the phone, she poked at it with her nose, bringing up a picture. "Look! Look!"

Bailey squinted at the screen. "What is it?" she wondered, but Simon had already come over to check.

"That is the most inane gift idea I have ever seen," he immediately began, but a stern look from Bailey silenced him.

"I am so glad you like it!" Shelby said happily. "Let's get it right now!"

Simon was flabbergasted at her lack of vocabulary knowledge, but he allowed that to pass for a more important question. "And how exactly do you intend to pay for this gift?"

"Oh, that's easy! You just put it in the car shop and click on play! I've seen my Ritchie boy do it millions of times!"

Bailey quickly stifled a laugh and ended up sneezing. Simon appeared to be holding himself from an apoplectic fit of rage.

"I might have gotten that backward," Shelby said, seeing their reactions and looking closer at the phone. "Maybe you play first and then put it in the car shop."

"I think you have been hanging out with the human pups too much, Shelby dear," Bailey said gently, wondering as an afterthought, "What do they teach pups in school these days?"

Simon coughed loudly and then spoke very articulately and with great exaggeration. "What she means to say is that the items are added to the *shopping cart* and that you are then required to click on *pay*. I do not know where the references to car shops and playing come in." Shaking his head, he said to Shelby without even gracing her with a look, "Where *did* you learn to read?"

Shelby opened her mouth to defend her reading abilities, but then they all heard The Man roaring from the other room.

"Never mind," said Simon swiftly, shoving the girls out of the way. "The Man is missing his phone." Quickly, he poked and prodded the device and then picked it up and trotted over to the couch, dropping it next to the TV remote.

Turning back to look at them, he said austerely, "The evil deed is done, and the gift shall arrive this Saturday, which is December the 15th, and the boys, as you call them, will be none the wiser, unless you blab your big mouth," adding the last for Shelby's benefit.

Shelby laughed and ran around the room.

Just then, Ritchie walked from around the corner and looked at her in surprise. "What are you doing, Miss Shelby?" Shelby stopped dancing and prancing around and went up to him sheepishly, but then he caught sight of The Man's phone on the couch. "Oh, there it is. We thought the kids were hiding it!"

Ritchie picked up the missing phone and turned to go, but then noticed that all the dogs were watching him intently. "You want to go outside again, already?" he said in surprise. Agreeable to that idea, they all got up and rushed to the door. Shaking his head, Ritchie followed them out, thinking with some disgust at the filthy state in which The Man allowed his phone to be.

That Friday evening, Shelby was so excited that she could hardly sleep at all and nearly kept Bailey up half the night. On Saturday, she nearly gave poor Simon a heart attack with her relentless teasing and antics. But the day came and went without sight or sign of the special package. Every time the back door to the store opened, Shelby went racing to see who it was, but the package never came. Both the UPS and FedEx guys came, but when she carefully examined the packages, the special gift was not enclosed.

On Sunday, Shelby was so depressed about the unexpected turn of events that she did not even want to eat, and even Simon began to feel a little sorry for her. Ritchie was very concerned and spent every spare moment next to her, but she would not be comforted.

After getting home from work that afternoon, The Man texted the vet to see if she had any ideas for the ailing dog, but it was Bailey who finally took matters into paw and solved the predicament.

Seeing how worried everyone looked, Bailey got up from lounging in her bed and began to poke and prod the miserable Shelby into a sitting position.

"You must stop this childish nonsense," Bailey gently growled. "These things happen all the time."

"But it's only nine days until Christmas," Shelby said miserably, trying to lie down again without Bailey's unkind teeth on her neck. "If it doesn't come in soon, Christmas will be *ruined*!"

"Nonsense," Bailey said firmly. "Now, come on. Can't you see how worried the humans are?"

Shelby looked up mournfully and saw that Ritchie was beside her, The Man was looking on from the couch, and even all the grandchildren were standing around, watching her with sad expressions on their faces. But she noticed Simon in his usual corner, staring at the dead beetle with a bit of a smirk on his face.

"Why isn't *he* upset?" Shelby asked, suddenly pouting.

"He has some ideas, you know," Bailey said.

"Well, why didn't he say so?!" Shelby said, getting up. She was a bit shaky from lack of sleep and lack of food, otherwise, she would have thrown herself at Simon in a rage. Instead, she simply gave a lurch and Ritchie reached out and caught her before she tripped and fell.

"Now, look at that," The Man said, quite pleased. "Good girl, Bailey."

"Are you feeling better, Miss Shelby?" Ritchie asked, offering her a treat.

Shelby felt a bit embarrassed at all the attention, but she accepted the treat, suddenly feeling hungry and wanting more. But she still had a bone to pick with Simon, who was still grinning in the corner at the beetle.

"I want to know the idea," Shelby said, impatiently to Bailey, trying to wriggle away from Ritchie.

"You must eat something, drink some water, and then go outside and walk around a bit," Bailey said firmly. "Then Simon and I will tell you the idea."

Shelby submitted to all the treatment and after an hour or two, the incident was forgotten and she was feeling back to her usual self.

"Now," Bailey said, stretching out luxuriously in her bed and turning her head to look at Shelby, "Simon will come and tell you all about the present and its travels."

"Simon will come—ha, ha," came back the sardonic reply from the couch where the little dog sat up next to The Man who was watching TV. "I think I am quite content up here, thank you very much."

Shelby looked around the room and then slipped out of her bed, creeping over to The Man and receiving a kind pat on the head. "Tell me, you meanie," she hissed up at Simon who was busily yawning and acting as if he was unaware of her presence.

"Tell you?" Simon said calmly with a regal air. "How about asking politely, you presumptuous insect?"

"Please tell me," Shelby said, rolling her eyes slightly.

"I saw that, minion," Simon said, looking down his nose at her.

Shelby sighed and lay down on the floor by The Man's feet. "I'm waiting," she said impatiently, but wagged her tail slightly, knowing she would get her way fairly soon.

After a few seconds, Simon stuck his nose over the edge of the couch and began his tale in a low voice. "The story is a bit of an odd one, but this is what happened. Your present, after it was ordered on Tuesday, came out of a warehouse in Texas the following day and was—"

"Texas? Where's that?" Shelby blurted out.

"I do not know exactly," Simon admitted, after harrumphing a bit from being interrupted. "But it is a large place, and it has a lot of guns, I do believe, at least according to your dear Ritchie." Seeing that the answer satisfied Shelby, he went on with his tale. "At that point, the United Parcel Service of America, commonly known as UPS—"

"I know what that is, you idiot!" Shelby interrupted again. "They are those guys with the boxes and the big trucks! I watch out for them all the time! Get on with the story!"

Simon immediately fell silent and appeared to be engrossed in the show that The Man was laughing at.

Shelby sat up and began to whine, causing The Man to look at her and pat her on the head again. She grinned as a jealous twinkle began to shine in one of Simon's eyes until it was a great gleam in both of his eyes and then she lay down again, knowing that she always got her way since she was the youngest and the cutest.

"And henceforth," Simon went on as if the latest interruption had never occurred, "the UPS delivered the package from Texas to Connecticut, which is another area that is much closer to our region," he hastily added so that he would not be stopped again. "And from there, it went to a facility in Massachusetts, which is even closer to here, but still not quite close enough."

"And then what?" Shelby asked, hanging on to every word that fell from the dog's arrogant snout.

"And then, well, the rest of the tale is a bit of a mystery. It appears that the United Parcel Service delivered the package to a facility belonging to the United States Postal Service—you know them also, they drive the little trucks all around the town, and the humans walk with a bag in the village—"

"Yes, yes, I know," Shelby said breathlessly, "but then what happened?"

"Certainly, I do not know. In fact, there is no one who knows," Simon said serenely, inclining his head slightly and closing his eyes. "The Postal Service received the package, but never marked it, and so it sits, somewhere in a forgotten bin, and who knows who shall discover it, when Christmas is passed, of course."

Shelby sat up, glaring at Simon. "You made that last part up, you meanie!"

"I did not," he replied, opening his eyes calmly. "See for yourself, if you can. Look up the tracking numbers on the mobile device on the nearby coffee table, if you be so bold." He closed his eyes again.

Shelby lay down again, feeling distressed. "Then what shall we do?" she mourned. "The boys will not get their present and Christmas will be a miserable failure!"

Simon glanced down at her and said cruelly, "I told you it was a ridiculous idea to begin with. Now what do you say?"

Shelby said nothing, but simply lay there with her chin on her paws, pouting. She remained like that for some time and then turned her head slightly to see Bailey snoozing happily in her bed. Getting up, she went over to Bailey and poked her with her wet nose.

"What will we do?" she said sadly to her sleeping friend. "Christmas will be ruined!"

Bailey opened her eyes slightly, yawned, and went right back to sleep.

Shelby turned away and headed out of the room, not even looking in Simon's direction, sensing that he was mocking her in her distress. She found Ritchie in his room, sitting at his desk and admiring one of his guns. She poked him with her cold nose and wished that he knew how to speak canine.

"Why, hello, Miss Shelby," Ritchie said politely, and she wagged her tail in response. He bent down and patted her on the head. "How are you feeling?"

Shelby sat down and handed him her paw, looking dolefully up at him and feeling sadder and sadder that his Christmas would be ruined.

"If you get a good night's sleep tonight, I'm sure you will be all better tomorrow," Ritchie said, turning back to his gun.

Shelby thought about that a moment as she sat next to him with her paw on his knee, and then she decided that would be a good idea. Turning away from him, she went and jumped up on his bed, making herself a little nest and then curling up for a nap.

Just before she dropped off to sleep, however, Shelby heard something that made her ears twitch. Lifting up her head, she caught a glimpse of a little black shadow at the door. She was inclined to jump down and bark, but then she saw a little black nose at the end of a little brown snout and put her head down with an aggravated sigh. It was just that miserable Simon come back to torture her dreams and prevent her from having a nice nap.

"I have an idea," she heard a whisper from the doorway.

Lifting her head, she looked at him directly, an idea of something deliciously rude to say popping into her mind, but the very thought made her feel guilty, and she wagged her tail apologetically.

Upon hearing her tail thumping on the bed, Ritchie turned and glanced at her, smiled to see her resting, and went back to his project.

"It is a good idea," Simon's voice came from the shadows. "I promise," he added.

"Well, what is this good idea?" she asked, her curiosity taking hold of her.

Creeping forward slightly so that she could see him in the doorway, Simon said, "Well, you know, the humans do not regularly expect presents from us canine creatures, so Christmas will not be ruined for *them*. It will only be ruined in a manner of speaking for those of us who understand that a part of it will be missing."

Shelby felt confused and shook her head slightly. "I don't get it," she said. "It will be ruined for me but not for the boys?"

"I wish you would cease referring to the humans as 'the boys'," Simon said in disgust.

"Why?" Shelby asked. "Aren't they boys?"

"Perhaps, in a manner of speaking, but you must remember that I am also, ahem, a boy."

"No, you're a dog," she said flippantly. "Anyway, answer the question, in a manner of speaking if you please, whatever that means."

"All right," Simon said with a patient sigh. "Technically, you are correct, but you must not consider that Christmas will be ruined for you entirely since *the boys* are planning to give you presents, and they will give one another presents so that no one will know that your present is missing."

"I will know," Shelby said. "And anyway, it's from all of us, not just me."

"Well, then," Simon said, suddenly feeling surprised at her generosity, "then, we can give it to them another time."

"Next Christmas?" Shelby said, beginning to be excited.

"No," Simon said quickly, but when he saw Shelby's ears droop, he added, "that is too far away. We can give it to them another holiday."

"What's another holiday?" Shelby wanted to know.

"New Year's Day, if it arrives in time. That is the next holiday after Christmas," he explained. "Or, if it takes even longer to arrive, then we can give it to them on Valentine's Day."

"Valentine's Day?" Shelby said in surprise. "You mean Candy Day?"

"Yes," Simon said, suddenly licking his lips. He looked longingly at a place in Ritchie's room where he knew there was a secret stash of snacks and treats. "I rather enjoy chocolate, as you may know."

"Yes, you're weird," Shelby said, suddenly feeling tired. "Go away, Simey, and goodnight."

Simon gave a contemptuous sniff. "How many times have I told you not to refer to me with that ridiculous title?"

"It fits you," she said sleepily. "And you need a nicer name anyway. Nicer than Sighhhh-Monnnn," she said his name in an exaggerated way to make it sound ugly. "Shelby, Bailey, Simey," she said with a long yawn. "That is nicer. Shel-by-Bai-ley-Si-mey—" and then, she was fast asleep.

12
Simon's Devilish Plan

A Holiday Tail, Part II

It was New Year's Day, and everyone was resting after a delicious dinner. Bailey was snoozing at The Man's feet, a growing puddle of drool at her nose. Shelby was happily gnawing on a piece of bone that she had hidden from Bailey for such a time as this. She did not exactly want to eat the bone, but she liked something to talk to when everyone else was sleeping or busy, and everyone was sleeping, except for grouchy old Simey, who was busily staring at a beetle in the corner. Why he liked that dead beetle, Shelby was sure that she would never even try to understand.

With a sigh, she put her nose down and began whispering to the bone about sunshine, green grass, and fluffy bunnies made out of snowballs.

A cough interrupted her daydream and Shelby's head immediately went up.

Simon was sitting nearby, not exactly watching her, but he had one ear slightly tilted in her direction.

Suddenly feeling excited, Shelby asked him, "Do you like snowball bunnies?"

At that, Simon looked straight at her. "I prefer killing snakes," he said in a cynical and arrogant tone.

Shelby gagged, thinking about how horrible snakes tasted. Rolling over on her side and extending a paw toward Simon, she whined, "Why are you so gross and nasty? Why can't you think about happy things?"

Simon fixed her with a cold stare. "I have more important things to consider than ridiculous objects like snowflakes, butterflies, and Christmas tinsel."

Shelby felt distracted by all those lovely things he just mentioned, but controlled herself, feeling that he had something else on his mind that he would presently reveal.

True to form, Simon went on. "In fact, I have a serious proposal regarding Operation Amazon, seeing as the surprise Christmas package has failed to arrive by the New Year's holiday."

Shelby was inclined to be confused, but she understood the words Amazon, package, and holiday, so she was delightfully excited. "What? What?" she demanded, sitting up and giving him her full attention.

An evil gleam shone in Simon's left eye, which was his stronger one. "To put it in the words of a certain powerful human, 'Let's give them hell.'"

Shelby looked at him with a bit of worried shock. "That's a bad word," she whispered.

Bailey's head suddenly shot up. "Who said a bad word?" she demanded sleepily.

"Simey did! Simey did!" Shelby cried out, jumping up and running over to Bailey. "Save me!"

Bailey sat up laboriously and glared at Simon.

Only too happy to get him in trouble, Shelby whispered, "He said he's going to give someone hell."

"I was quoting a certain powerful human," Simon said, rolling his eyes. "You are too sheltered."

"I am not! I am not!" Shelby protested, but then, seeing that Bailey was lying down again with a flop, she asked, "What's sheltered?"

Bailey yawned. "It means that you don't understand a good word from a bad word, dear, that's all." She closed her eyes but then looked up and blinked. "Simon was quoting The Man, that's all."

"That is precisely what I said one moment ago, you dimwit," Simon burst in, glaring at Shelby.

Bailey growled slightly and then dropped off to sleep again, just as The Man stirred and nudged Bailey with his foot as if to comfort her because of a nightmare.

Shelby tentatively returned to her bed and lay down with a sigh. She glanced up at Simon who was evidently gloating.

"Well, would you like to hear my plan?" he asked after a moment.

"Okay," Shelby said noncommittally.

"We track down those crooks who confiscated our present for the humans and make them pay!" Simon said with malicious delight.

Shelby put her head up. "How?"

"Go fetch the mobile device and I shall demonstrate," he replied.

Shelby rose slowly, looking up tentatively at The Man as he reclined on the couch. She stopped next to Bailey and pretended to poke the sleeping dog with her nose, but then quickly put her head up, snatched The Man's phone, and ran back to Simon, dropping it at his feet and wagging her tail furiously.

He wagged his tail slightly in response but then sat down and settled down to business. After a few moments, he put up his head to find Shelby whispering to her bone fragment about packages and surprises.

"Now stop chattering with that rawhide and look here," he said superciliously, "the package is still being held hostage in the

Commonwealth of Massachusetts, so our decision at this time must be for quick and firm action."

"Okay," Shelby said distractedly. "What does that mean?"

"Listen to this," Simon said with a devilish grin. "This letter will frighten them indeed." Then he proceeded to read his missive.

> Hated Lords and Ladies of the Realm of Humans,
>
> Be duly advised that your shipment has not been delivered as scheduled and promised. For that cause, I am conferring with my attorney and will have a warrant prepared for your arrest within 24 hours. Deliver the goods or your lives are at stake.
>
> Maliciously,
> A Disgruntled Customer

Shelby gazed at Simon in awe. "You have your own attorney?"

"No, silly," Simon said in exasperation, "but we are threatening them, remember?"

"Oh, but isn't that lying?" Shelby wondered.

Bailey raised her head. "Who is lying?" she demanded.

Shelby leaped up, hid the bone, and ran over. "He is! He is! I'm not! I would never lie! Save me!"

Simon rolled his eyes and sat up straight and tall as he ever could, steeling himself against Bailey's reprimand.

But Bailey simply yawned and lay down again. "Shelby, dear, as long as you do not do anything wrong, then you have nothing to worry about."

"But—but—but what about Simon?" Shelby whimpered.

"He is none of your business," Bailey replied. "If he tries to make you do anything bad, then let me know, and I'll settle his hash, but otherwise, you have nothing to worry about. He is his own dog, after all."

"Okay," Shelby replied, returning to her mat and lying down again. She wagged her tail a bit guiltily at Simon, but he lay down as well and ignored her. Soon, the only noises present were snores and the TV in the background.

"So, returning to our business at hand," Simon began, but he was interrupted by the sound of Shelby crunching on a corner of leftover bone. "I see how it is," he said, eyebrows raised.

"How what is?" she asked innocently.

"You are adamantly against cursing and swearing and lying and bluffing, but you are certainly in favor of stealing, hmmmm?"

Shelby immediately hid the bone and put her nose in the air. "I didn't steal it! I'm only saving it for later when Bailey is hungry again! And anyway, it was lonely, so I'm telling it stories and keeping it company!"

"So I see," Simon said haughtily, but then he grinned, "O my child, I am pleased to see you learning."

"Your child? I am not your child!" Shelby protested. "Do I look like a fat pink baby to you?"

"I only mean child in a manner of speaking," Simon returned arrogantly. "But let us return to our business at hand, shall we?"

"Shall we," Shelby said, imitating him. But she did not like that. "We shall? We will? Shall we? Will we?" She said, trying each out in turn. "Which is it?" she finally asked, shaking her head as if a bee was in one ear.

"Never mind such nonsense," Simon said bitterly. "Try to concentrate on the case at hand! Now, I have edited the letter slightly, so let me read it again."

"No, no," Shelby said quickly, "I don't want to hear it again. It is hideously frightful, and it even threatens me." She cradled her bone fragment between her paws.

"Excellent," Simon said, quite pleased. "Then I am certain that it will serve its purpose well. I will send it immediately." Just as he bent his nose to hit send, his sharp ears caught a sound and he dropped the phone, rushing as fast as he could to the front door and barking furiously.

Shelby and Bailey followed him, a bit puzzled but eager to discover the reason for his actions. Just that moment, Ritchie walked in, coming back from a visit with his family.

"Hello," he said, not at all surprised to see the dogs staring up at him. "Do you want to go outside?"

Bailey and Shelby happily agreed, but Simon appeared to be interested in returning to the living room. Before he could turn around, however, the two larger females steamrolled him out the door and a wild game of chase and tag ensued.

After five minutes, Shelby suddenly stopped and remembered something.

"A package!" she said with excitement.

"Where?" Bailey wondered, looking around.

"Ritchie! He had one!" Shelby rushed to the door. "It must have worked!"

"What worked?" Bailey asked, following her. She looked sideways at Simon, who still appeared nonplussed from the steamrolling incident. "What is this all about?" she demanded.

"Let me in! Let me in!" Shelby cried at the door, and as if he heard her plainly, Ritchie opened the door and they all tumbled in.

Simon went rushing into the living room, only to find The Man picking up his phone from the floor as he told Ritchie that he had heard about an incoming cold front on the news.

Bailey was rather perplexed by the happenings, so she left the room to go get a drink from the nearest toilet.

But Shelby was so happy that she began leaping around, trying to jump up on a chair and reach a small brown box that Ritchie had put on the table only minutes ago.

"What are you doing, Miss Shelby?" Ritchie asked, looking at her antics in a bit of amused bewilderment. "You want this box?"

He picked it up and looked at it as Shelby danced around him in excitement.

"Open it! Open it!" she said in delight.

"It's for you," Ritchie said to The Man as the latter followed him in from the living room.

"Merry Christmas!" Shelby shouted ecstatically, running around the room. Bailey, coming back from the bathroom, grabbed the younger canine by the ear, and they began play-fighting.

Meanwhile, The Man was opening the box. "Where did this come from?" he wondered as he looked inside, finding a rather detailed snowglobe with a country landscape of a great big house and several dogs running outside in the yard. "I didn't order this, did you?"

Ritchie came over from the sink and glanced into the box. "I have no idea," he said, just as perplexed.

"Do you like it? Isn't it beautiful?" Shelby cried happily, pulling away from Bailey and rushing toward them. "We got it to surprise you! Merry Christmas!"

"Well, it's kind of nice," The Man admitted. "It would look fine on the mantel."

"Yeah, that is actually really cool," Ritchie agreed. "Are you sure you didn't order it?"

The Man fixed him with a beady stare. "I was about to ask you the same thing. I'm going to check my Amazon account."

"It was Simon! From all of us!" Shelby shouted.

"How many times do I have to tell you," Bailey said, grabbing her ear again. "They can't understand Dog. Now pipe down!"

Shelby tore away from Bailey and rushed into the living room to find Simon. "It worked! It worked!" she said jubilantly. "Your nasty letter worked!"

"It did not," he said sourly, sitting in his old corner and staring at the dead beetle.

"What do you mean?" Shelby said in surprise, settling down, though her tail still wagged in determination. "They got the package right after you sent the letter!"

"No," Simon said angrily. "I never sent it."

Shelby was astonished. "You didn't? Why not?"

"I was prevented from doing so," he said bitterly. "I heard your dear Ritchie coming up the driveway in his truck and dropped the phone, and then we all ran out, and then before I could return and send it, you dimwits crowded me out the door, and then when we *finally* came back in, a certain powerful human woke up and picked up his phone before I could do anything further."

Shelby gulped. "Did he see the message?"

"No," Simon said. "He cleared it and closed the page before he realized what he was doing. He was just waking up, after all."

"Well, then what do we do?" Shelby wondered.

"Consider it a successful mission in terms of the purchase, but a failed experiment in terms of bullying the customer service representatives," Simon said bitterly.

Shelby sat there sadly for a moment and then began to creep away. She heard The Man talking to Bailey and Ritchie in the other room and felt even sadder that they were so happy and Simon was so cranky.

At that moment, The Man's phone beeped and he looked at the newly-arrived email.

"We hope you had a good Amazon experience," he read and then deleted it with some choice words about how creepy the internet was these days.

Suddenly, Shelby was struck with a happy realization and she whirled around, running back to Simon and his dead beetle.

"You are a genius!" she said exuberantly. "Just think! You only had to write out the nasty email and it worked!"

"What nonsense are you talking about?" he said sourly.

"You didn't even have to send it! Just by typing it out, it scared them into sending the package!"

Simon felt skeptical about that at first, but as Shelby continued to explain it to him, he was convinced. Sitting upright with a supercilious grin, he remarked, "So *that's* why humans always talk about attorneys—it gets immediate results!"

"Yes!" Shelby said happily and was about to say more when they both heard a familiar sound from the kitchen. It was the delicious noise of food rolling into doggy dishes.

"Guys," The Man said needlessly, "it's time to eat!"

The End

13
Crooks, Swindlers, and Thieves

Danielle and Jessica Jones were sisters, having grown up together in an adventure-loving household where they learned to stick together through thick and thin. After moving out of the house, going through college, and beginning their own careers, they settled in a comfortable apartment together, carrying on their tradition of being roommates that began when the two of them were but toddlers.

One of their adventures together happened on a crazy summer day toward the end of August, when they each took off from their respective jobs for a much-needed and well-deserved break—Dani from her dispatching job at the county emergency services and Jess from her accounting duties at a private firm in town.

Though the sisters saw each other every day, it was rare for them to deliberately request vacation days. and it was even rarer for them to take time off together, but they committed to go hiking together on a certain Monday, two weeks before Labor Day.

Jess did not care where they went, as long as it was outside. Dani particularly wanted to put her name in the book at the tallest fire tower in the region, which stood proudly on top of the local Mount Eberle. The tower was rarely used as much as it had once been but stood monument to the old-fashioned methods of forest care and preservation.

"Zak told me he might be on shift," Dani said with a gleam in her eye as she settled into the passenger seat in her sister's car.

Jess, used to Dani's name-dropping and knowing there was no reason to inquire further about the fellow mentioned, simply started the vehicle and they coasted out of the driveway. But she did suggest after a moment, "Why don't you text him and find out?"

"Ha!" Dani laughed and then explained, "No cell service up there. And we civilians aren't allowed access to their radio frequency." Then she chuckled. "Though, of course, as a dispatcher, I have means and ways of figuring these things out."

"You and your means and ways!" Jess laughed slightly in response, shaking her head with amusement but admitting aloud that she honestly did not care. "As long as we are outside in the fresh air with no responsibilities to distract us, then I'm perfectly happy."

"Yes, I bet you didn't even bring your phone," Dani teased, knowing how much her sister did not like being at the beck and call of others.

"No, I didn't," Jess readily admitted. "I have a 911 operator with me, who has plenty of gadgets and communication devices, so why would I bother?"

It was a quiet drive for the most part, but as they approached exit signs pointing toward a town named Milford, Jess casually mentioned that she wanted to briefly stop at a place not too far off the thoroughfare since there was a branch store owned by one of her clients that she had wished to visit for some time.

"This is a non-business trip!" Dani chided.

"It is purely for my own amusement!" Jess returned.

"So you say now until you start chatting up the manager, and he ropes you into another job!"

"I do not chat," Jess said scornfully, "that sounds more like you."

And so they went back and forth for another few minutes or so, but when they arrived at Exit 38, they pulled off, both in agreement about the brief stop.

A couple of miles off the thoroughfare, Jess turned the car into the parking lot of a lawn and garden store.

"You can stay if you wish," Jess said to Dani, holding out her ring of keys.

Dani grabbed it, but then said, "Nah, I'll take a look around, too. Looks like a decent place."

"Suit yourself." Jess stepped out and headed for the front door. Last she saw, Dani was heading toward the rows of fruit trees off to the side.

To her surprise, when Jess walked into the store and turned down an aisle, she immediately spotted Robert Q. Roberts crouching down in front of a locked knife display. Swiftly, she backtracked, but not before he glanced her way. Whether or not he recognized her was another thing altogether, but she took no chances.

Robert Q. Roberts, or "Bobby Q.," as he was often nicknamed, was something of a business felon in her circles, popular as a fraud, a cheat, a blackmailer, and a liar, but there was no paper trail anywhere to prove it. Jess had crossed paths with him a couple of times in accounting, usually trying to fix a problem for her clients that had been a scam. She still felt a chill every time she saw him, even though he was not necessarily a personal threat to her.

"May I help you, miss?" a pot-bellied fellow asked Jess, and she glanced at him, feeling instinctively that he was a person of authority in that establishment but not knowing whether or not she could trust him.

She slowly began, "Well, I—"

But at that moment, Robert Q. Roberts came around the corner and grinned his oily grin straight at her.

"So it was you!" he said in a smarmy tone as a blush began to creep across her face. "I thought I recognized that walk! But you know what really did it?" he said, turning to the store owner, "It was the hair," he said with an evil chuckle. "Do you know how much I can tell about a person from their hair?" he went on.

Jess immediately lost interest and turned to walk out the door. She had already heard all of his stories, all of his claims to fame, all of his boastful remarks. They were all the same, and he repeated the same stories over and over to everyone that he encountered.

"Oh, no, you don't!" Bobby Q. said, running around her to stand between her and the door. Chuckling again, he looked past her to the manager, who appeared a bit confused. A couple of other employees began to appear, gathering around in curiosity.

Knowing that it would become a true spectacle if she allowed it to carry on, Jess began to edge toward the nearest aisle, as Bobby Q.'s braggadocious voice began to tell the famous tale about him and a bald senator from Chicago and the flight they shared in a trip to DC. She mentally began rehearsing her report back to her boss back at the office.

"Stopped in at Milford's Town and Country store. Saw Bobby Q. and realized it was his territory. Promptly left."

Jess sighed silently, glanced to her left, and then swiftly rounded the corner of the aisle, heading straight to the back of the store.

She thought she had escaped detection when she suddenly heard him squall out, "Now where'd that silly girl head off to?"

Neatly avoiding a man walking toward her, Jess broke into a brisk walk and turned down another aisle where a young fellow was tossing bags of chicken feed from a cart onto the nearby racks. She slowed, and the young fellow looked at her.

"I'm sorry, can you point me toward the nearest exit?" she asked, glancing back over her shoulder.

"The front door—the one you came in," he replied, appearing a bit perplexed.

She imagined she could hear Bobby Q.'s voice. "Hello? Where'd you go, silly girl?"

She looked at the young man again. "Trying to avoid a stalker, embarrassingly enough," she admitted.

He put down the next bag he had begun to lift and kind of laughed. Then, "Follow me," and without further comment, he led the way to the back of the warehouse and the employee exit.

"I see you," the smarmy voice said somewhere behind them, but he, in fact, did not see them. By the time Jess was out of the back door, Roberts had encountered a door that was clearly labeled "Employees Only." Roberts might be disgusting but he was not stupid. So, turning on heel, he headed back to the front door.

Meanwhile, Jess thanked the young man, walked through the yard past several more curious employees, and found Dani standing by a truck, chatting with a bearded fellow with hunting and fishing decals on his cab windows. He stopped talking when Jess approached.

Dani turned to see what had happened and grinned to see her sister, "Hey, ready to go?" She unhooked the car keys from her belt and held them out to her sister.

Jess glanced toward the store's main entrance, expecting Robert Q. Roberts to burst out at any second. "Yes, sorry to interrupt but—" She hesitated and glanced at the door again. Then she looked at Dani.

"Trouble is brewing." She looked at the country fellow. "Hello," she said politely, seeing that he was still staring at her, and then followed it up with a matter-of-fact, "Goodbye."

Taking the keys, Jess went to her car and got in, starting it up just as Roberts barreled out of the store and spotted her. Jess glanced a bit impatiently at Dani, seeing that she was shaking hands with the rugged truck owner, but was taking her sweet time in doing so.

Bobby Q. strutted up to her car, put his hands on his hips, and stood nearby, beginning to mock her through the window.

Jess ignored him as much as she could, considering turning the radio on to drown out his tirade of mockery or driving over to Dani, but instead, she listened carefully to what Bobby Q. was saying and wished she had her phone to record his crazy speech. She was not, after all, as desperate as he appeared to be.

Meanwhile, Dani was walking her way, straight toward Bobby Q. with a curious look on her face. "Hey, what's up?" she asked, looking at Bobby Q. with her right eyebrow slightly up.

He appeared to diminish slightly with her no-nonsense question, but just as he was about to take off again, Dani walked around him and got into the car. At that, Bobby Q. seemed surprised, and then he laughed, beginning to take out his phone.

"Obviously," Dani said as she slammed the door and took out her own phone to snap a picture of him, "that creep has no brains at all."

"That creep, as you call him," Jess said quietly, taking her time in backing her car out of the parking space, "is none other than Robert Q. Roberts."

"Haha!" Dani said with astonished laughter, snapping a couple of extra pictures for good measure of the man she had heard plenty about as they slowly drove back toward the main road. "Well, that's a shocker. I definitely did not expect him to look like that!"

"You expect crooks, swindlers, and thieves to be attractive?" Jess wondered mildly. "But obviously, he doesn't know you, so that is good, at least. Did he take your photo, too?"

"No clue," Dani said, reviewing the pictures she had taken. She already knew plenty about Robert Q. Roberts, and she suddenly felt that she had enough of him for one day, so she switched gears.

"You'd like this story." So she launched into a description of the redneck fellow she had been chatting up, who apparently worked in the hill country for one of their uncles some years ago, but recently relocated and was starting a Christmas tree farm.

"That's good," Jess said, as they pulled back onto the thoroughfare. "At least you made another connection, even though you accused me of almost getting roped into another job!"

Dani laughed but felt quite proud of herself.

Jess sighed slightly. "And now for the real adventure. I am glad to be away from the crazy people once again."

It was a beautiful day. The sun was shining, the birds were singing, the wind was softly blowing through the treetops, and the women arrived at their destination within record time. Leaving their car, the two of them went on a long hike up to the fire tower.

The hike was pleasant and uneventful. The sisters talked some but mostly enjoyed the peace and quiet of the trails and seeing numerous birds and creatures among all the mature foliage. They went up to the top of the fire tower and Dani happily put her name in the book, taking a picture of it to send to her pals once they were back in cell service range.

Jess decided to pass on the honor, but Dani was insistent.

"Oh come on," Dani said, holding the pen out to her. "Just sign it!"

"It's fine," her sister replied with a shrug, "you go ahead."

"What's the matter? This is a once-in-a-lifetime opportunity!"

Jess laughed. "If I really wanted to write my name in this book, I can always come up here another time. Go ahead, write my name in it if you feel that strongly about it."

"Oh, good grief," Dani said, jotting down her sister's name and dating it. "Well, let's go down to the radio station and see if anyone's there. And then how about some lunch?"

"Good plan," Jess said, so they took the path down to the radio station and soon ran into a ranger named Carly. Zak was not around, as he was assigned to the North Country that day, but Dani enjoyed chatting with Carly for a bit while Jess set out their picnic lunch nearby.

After a quiet and peaceful lunch, the two of them continued on the trails on the west side of the mountain, and then headed all the way back to their parking area, a bit tired but happy and content.

As they approached the vehicle, Jess seemed to drag, even though the paths were still all downhill at that point.

"You tired?" Dani wondered, reaching for her water.

"Nah," Jess replied, making some brief comment about being loathe to leave the peace of the wilderness for the wilds of civilization.

Dani gave a contemptuous sniff at that point, saying that civilization was preferable to animal life.

"Maybe so," Jess admitted, but at least they don't deal with bills!"

On the drive back, Dani took a short nap, since Jess was adamant that she was not tired. When Jess pulled onto Route 30, which was the back way of driving into their town, Dani's phone began to beep.

Dani woke up and stretched. "Ah, cell service again!" She began to happily review her texts and send her a picture of her name in the fire tower guest book when she laughed.

"Look at that, Zak texted me. And Josh!"

"Josh our cousin?"

"Yes, and he said that he gave my number to Pete, the Christmas tree guy I was talking to." Dani laughed at that. "Josh apparently didn't know that I already gave Pete my number."

"Everyone has your number," Jess said a bit sarcastically.

"The more the merrier!" Dani replied happily and then began to tell a tale about how she had given her number to a co-worker, but then another fellow with nefarious purposes decided to ask her for it as well, and how she had to confront him to tell him the business.

A couple of miles down the road, Dani stopped talking to look at her sister who was steadily driving. "Obviously, you're not very interested. That Bobby Q. idiot back on your mind?"

"No, go on," Jess said, glancing back into the rearview mirror. "I am interested, and I'm listening to every word. In fact, it sounds like something that my friend Jenna went through, too, but I've just been watching that car behind us. It keeps swerving back and forth."

"Aha!" Dani said, turning to look behind them, always interested in possibly dangerous drivers that could result in emergency situations. "Oh, nothing to worry about," she said, shrugging and turning back to the front. "Just a new driver."

"Nice," Jess said snidely, slowing slightly for a bit of traffic ahead.

"I guess," Dani agreed, "but she definitely hasn't been on the road that long if she drives like that." Turning around again, she pulled her phone out and began to make a note about the car's information. "I got a call about a reckless driver the other day that took about three troopers to pull him over."

The traffic was picking up now, and the car was on their tail. Jess glanced at Dani again. "Well, where's your police friends when you need them?" She looked behind them again as they stopped at a red light behind a Chevy truck.

"Where are we? Glenville or Scottstown? Or one of the little hamlets in between? I should text Joe and see if he's in the area," Dani replied. "I think this is his district."

"I think we just left Glenville," Jess said.

Dani glanced back again and laughed. "Well, the new driver actually has an instructor! I know this dude—he's the worst in the county!"

"Oh, brother," Jess said in a bored tone.

Dani sank down into her seat as she began to text her friend Joe. She began to wonder out loud if the Scottstown Gun Shop had some good deals on ammunition.

"Probably," Jess said quietly, beginning to gas the engine now that the light was green and traffic was slowly moving forward, "but didn't you check that out already? I thought you and Sam and Kate went shooting up in Clearview earlier this summer and passed through here."

"Yeah, we did, but we brought our—whoa!" Dani sat straight up in her seat, watching as the rusty blue car that had been behind them suddenly whizzed around them and started weaving in and out of traffic. "I'm calling 911!"

"You do that," Jess said calmly as she drove on steadily, but she did not take her eyes off the car, which was busily careening into a nearby ditch and then attempting to back out as traffic slowed and went around the wrecker cautiously.

Dani had the phone on speaker and was busily chattering away as she waited for the call to be received. "The instructor was driving this time, but how he got into the driver's seat while we were only stopped for a moment—I need a crossroad! I need a crossroad!"

"Here's your crossroad," Jess said calmly, neatly swerving to the left and pulling onto a rough road called Fairview Street. She did a U-turn so they were facing traffic, and watched as the reckless driver continued to demolish the vehicle by trying to ram his way out of the rocky ditch.

"County 911, where's the location of your emergency?" the call finally picked up.

"Heyyy, Tommy!" Dani replied in an overly friendly, exaggerated tone.

Jess's head whipped around, and she stared at her sister in shock as the two of them began chatting it up over the line. Certainly, this was not the way to be talking during an emergency call! But Tommy was replying in like tone, kidding Dani about not being able to stay away from him, even on her day off.

Jess began to wonder how on earth this was going to go down, but Dani changed her tune just as quickly.

"Hey, man, I got a guy on Route 30 driving in and out of a ditch, crossroads of Fairview Street and Route 52. He was driving recklessly and sitting on our tail for a few miles, and then he really took off after the light, intersection with Route 52."

"Really!" Tommy said, all ears. "Description?"

"Beat up blue Ford Taurus," Dani said, "license plate Lincoln X-ray 2-2-3-3. But get this—it's Joe Price who crashed, and he was supposed to be teaching some chick how to drive!"

"Great," Tommy said, "I'll send Pete and Jackie over." And that was that.

Dani put down the phone with a look of glee.

"What was that?" Jess said in dismay, still staring at her sister while taking time to glance in front and behind to make sure she was not blocking traffic.

Dani looked at her with a chuckle. "Me and Tommy?"

"How unprofessional can you be?" Jess demanded. "And aren't they recording all your calls?"

"Oh, sure," Dani said casually, "but no one listens to anything. And Tommy and I go way back, so you know."

"I'm sure I *don't* know," Jess replied, "but I'm *not* sure I even want to understand."

"Cheer up," Dani said genially, pointing down toward the light. "Look! Here comes Pete!"

"You going to get out and talk to him?"

"Nah, he's a little weird. I might say hi to Jackie, though. She's cool," Dani said. She sat there, a large grin plastered on her face as she watched the second police car roll in, one officer redirecting traffic while the other stopped the perpetrators of the traffic incident and began giving them a citation.

"Well, look at that," Dani said after a moment, seeing both the man and the woman being escorted out of their vehicle. "I bet it's being impounded for lack of registration and probably lack of proper identification to boot. Just what Joe deserves."

They sat there for a few more moments, watching the scene, and Dani began wondering aloud who would pick up the pair when a run-down Buick coasted over behind Jackie's troop vehicle and parked.

"Who is that?" Dani wondered.

"I have an odd feeling," Jess said, a wrinkle appearing on her forehead. "It reminds me of—"

"Well, I think I'm going to check it out and go say hi to Jackie," Dani said impatiently, unbuckling and starting to open the car door.

"Wait!" Jess said, recognizing a face in the car window. "Get down!" But it was too late. Out of the driver's window, a smarmy face appeared and began to grin larger and larger as he caught sight of the two women across the road.

"Robert Q. Roberts!" the two women cried out in unison.

"I'm not afraid of him," Dani added with a laugh.

Jess groaned slightly and shook her head. "It's not about fear, dummy. It's about being on the good side of the law. They told me he was involved in oversight for impoundments and even went so far as to scam new drivers and so on, but I didn't believe them."

"Who told you?" Dani wondered.

"Someone who apparently knows what they are talking about!" Jess said, still disgusted. "You still gonna go out there and say hello to Jackie? If you do, I might just tag along and give him a piece of my mind."

Dani laughed at that, and then quietly buckled herself back in as they watched Bobby Q. get out of the car and start talking to Matt in an animated way, motioning to the two individuals that had been escorted to Jackie's car. "If they call for backup, then I'll go out there, but at this point, I would only get in the way."

Every so often, Matt's face turned a darker shade of pink and Bobby Q. would turn and grin a bit larger in the direction of Jess and Dani.

"Did you ever wonder if faces could split wide open from grinning so evilly?" Jess wondered.

Dani snorted. "No, but his could if anyone's could." She glanced at the clock. "Hey, I'm going to miss my meeting at the club if we don't start heading out now."

Jess obligingly shifted the car back into drive and joked, "And miss the show of Bobby Q. and the cops?"

"No, thank you, I'm good," Dani replied, settling down to text one of her friends.

"It was a good day," Jess reflected as they passed the scene and merged back into normal traffic. Bobby Q. and his antics notwithstanding."

"Still is!" Dani replied. "The day's not over. How about you come with us to the club? We're going over a couple of things, which shouldn't take more than an hour, and then we're going out to the steakhouse for supper."

"Well," Jess hesitated, thinking about her books and writing projects that she was looking forward to resuming.

"Come on," her sister said. "They have a good spread, and they're not that expensive either. And I can pay!"

"Money's not an issue," Jess scoffed. "I'm an accountant, after all."

"Good, then you have no excuse," Dani said happily. "I should tell Mom. She'd be happy, too, and I'll introduce you to some guys, too."

"No, thank you," Jess said firmly.

"Okay, I'll introduce them to you, but not the other way around," Dani said in just as firm a tone.

Jess laughed. "All right, I'll come, but I'm not staying out past 10!"

"10?" Dani said, disbelief dripping from her tone.

"10:30?" Jess said, beginning to feel a bit concerned.

"Don't worry, we'll be home by 9," Dani said with a laugh. She glanced behind them, looked back at her phone, and then laughed again. "What a great day! And this is going to be an awesome night!"

Please Leave a Review

If you enjoyed reading *Adventures Are Everywhere*, then please be kind and leave a review on the site from which you purchased the book. Book reviews greatly help both authors and readers, and I look forward to hearing what you thought about my collection!

Read More

Before you go, check out the following sample from my second book, *Faithless Friends and Replacement Lovers: Short Stories about Love and Loss*, available on Amazon and other major online distributors.

The Preposterous Proposal

A long time ago in Bonny Old England, there was a fine but rather preposterous knight named Sir John Sebastian Dudley. His most defining characteristic was demonstrating a great fluctuation of emotions in a way not at all befitting a man of his stead. Oftentimes, he found himself in perilous scraps because of his inability to control his fits, rages, whims, and fancies. Other times, he neatly escaped by the mere kindness of his comrades and boasted that it was he who had rescued himself from peril by his own wit and merit.

In the springtime of his thirtieth year, Sir Dudley was called to the front line of battle for his king. After settling his affairs and preparing for the journey in obedience to the throne, he rode off on his most trusted steed with many a romantic thought about how gloriously he would bring the war to a victorious close for his country.

Shortly after his departure, Dudley chanced to fall into company with a group of excellent fellows on a dangerous mission of which they would speak nothing. Pressed by curiosity, Dudley was determined to learn something of their secret quest and thus plagued the group every day with various and sundry offers of service.

For a whole week, the noble company rebuffed Dudley's unsubtle suggestions, but they soon tired of his fanciful words and plotted a scheme to rid themselves of him altogether. As they expected to arrive upon the scene of war within three days' time, the excellent group swiftly set their plot in motion by inviting Dudley to give particular care and attention to a young fellow in their company who would not be directly engaged in battle.

At first, Sir Dudley felt offended at their offer, thinking he was far better than acting the nursemaid to an inexperienced youth who was sure to flee at the first sign of a bloody skirmish. After further consideration, however, he recalled how deliberately the group of nobles respected the young fellow. Presuming this was due to the lad having a prestigious background, Dudley concluded that any good deed done for the young man would certainly result in a bountiful reward.

From there, Dudley was all too happy to comply with the group's wishes, promising to bear young O'Reilly henceforth in safety. Having succeeded at their plot, the noblemen bid a hearty farewell to the young fellow and beat a hasty retreat, leaving Dudley and O'Reilly quite to themselves.

As it was nearing evening, Dudley suggested they make camp for the night, offering to take care of the fire and nightly sup while pointing out a fine grassy spot for the young noble to take his rest. O'Reilly complied in silence, spending much of the evening in quiet reflection and waiting until the sun had gone down to remove his armor and bid Dudley a good night.

Upon the morrow, the two fellows resumed their travels, making quite a motley pair and creating a fine topic for gossip as they wound through the little villages and towns toward the scene of battle. Indeed, a goodly number of villagers and townsfolk wondered at their appearance, for the two diligently rode by at a rapid pace without a single word to one another or to anyone else, putting their poor horses at danger of wearing down before they even reached the war.

On Dudley's part, he felt sorely irritated at O'Reilly for being a measly fellow without the stomach for good food, fine drink, and comfortable living. After all, Dudley had awoken with a fine thought and presented it to his companion.

"Let us ride far today, my good man, and tonight we will dine in comfort and sleep at the finest of inns in Millersville," he told O'Reilly as they saddled up for the day.

"Nay, but we will follow the main road through Dunshire and arrive at battle by noon tomorrow," O'Reilly replied, wise to Dudley's scheme to bypass the poverty-stricken towns and head further north than necessary.

The two knights, thus being at odds, spent much of the day in silence. Upon reaching the crossroads leading to a westerly road or the northern path, the pair came to a halt and Dudley began to wheedle.

"Think ye about the goodly time we would have, what with the fine inn owned by my friend Alan and his kin. What has any scurvy town by comparison but a rowdy lot that would surely meet your disdain?"

"We shall go on as planned, for 'tis on the main path leading to the west, and we may surely camp solitary if the company displeases you," O'Reilly said without hesitation, his youthful voice certain beneath his helmet.

Growling in irritation, Dudley jerked his horse's head in the intended direction and returned to his former silence for the remainder of the day. Only when they reached the last village just beyond the battlefield did he recover his tongue, doing his best to find merriment in food and drink that evening.

As for O'Reilly, while his companion found solace from the upcoming conflict in strong liquor and deep sleep, this young fellow was occupied in more noble preparations, much to the admiration of the others present.

The morning sun rose early and red in the eastern sky, bidding the two knights rise and join the king's army in battle. O'Reilly remained as cheerful and complacent as always as they broke their fast, loaded their goods upon O'Reilly's horse, and went forward on foot, but Dudley was in quite an irascible temper.

"I tell you," Knight Dudley fumed, his memory going back to the trivialities of the day prior, "as if I had not told you a hundred times over, the proper path leads round about to Millersville and not on this poor road that now directs us across the grassy mount yonder."

"Be that as it may," responded his companion, "the battle is before us now, and there is no turning back, though it may be seemly for you to think otherwise."

Dudley was not finished with his complaints. "Were it not for my goodly steed having been stolen in the night, we would be in the battle now as we speak!"

"Ah, yes, your goodly steed," said O'Reilly, reflectively, pausing by a tuft of grass. "Well, truth be told, I loaned him to a passing knight for a small token of silver when you were asleep."

"You!" Dudley's voice and visage were now all full of wrath. "You sold my fair Philip!"

"Nay, loaned," corrected the other, ignoring the rage and plodding on. "The knight had greater need than you or I at the time, and when we reach the other side of this fine field, and supposing that neither knight nor horse has yet perished, you shall have your fair Philip back again."

Read **_Faithless Friends and Replacement Lovers: Short Stories About Love and Loss_** to learn what happens next.

About the Author

The author manages Elizabeth's Writing Corner, where she reads, writes, edits, and coaches aspiring authors. A true Renaissance woman, she enjoys cooking, gardening, hiking, painting, and playing music in addition to taking care of her family. She hopes to publish more books in the future and would love to hear from you about your stories and adventures. Contact her directly by visiting her website at https://www.elizabethswritingcorner.com.